"Sexual attraction is raw and immediate..."

"It's about a man and a woman," Rob said, tracing his fingers along the line of Hailey's jaw. "The feel of her skin, the way she smells." His voice dropped to a near whisper. "The way she tastes."

And he closed the short distance between them and put his mouth on hers.

Nothing could have prepared Hailey for the lust that punched through her system. A light, teasing kiss turned hungry and hot in a nanosecond. She made a little moaning sound in the back of her throat as she reached for him, wanting to feel the solid outline of his chest. His tongue teased and tormented her. She'd never been kissed like this. Never imagined anything close to this.

He kissed her for seven eternities, taking his time, not trying to rip off her clothes or talk her into his bed, but kissing her as though his whole existence depended on nothing but this moment.

Getting involved with Rob wasn't on her agenda, but she knew that she'd been seriously compromised.

When he pulled slowly away from her, he grinned at her wryly.

"You can't get *that* on the internet...."

Dear Reader,

I confess, I love those real estate shows on television. I love the ones where we follow a couple as they try to pick the perfect home, I love the ones where decorators turn disasters into showplaces. I even love looking at real estate listings in cities where I know I will never live.

I suspect I'm not alone, given the popularity of real estate shows on TV, the constant talk about where the market is and where it's going. I think the fun is in the fantasy that that home could be yours. That couple squabbling over an extra bedroom versus a bigger yard could be you. So I set out to write a book where a Realtor falls in love, not only with the home she's listed, but most inconveniently, with the guy who is selling it. And in particular with one big, beautiful four-poster bed in the master bedroom.

I hope you enjoy Hailey and Rob's story, and get a little vicarious pleasure out of the story of how the wrong man in the wrong bed turns out to be exactly the right man in the right bed.

I love hearing from readers. Visit me on the web at www.nancywarren.net.

Happy reading,

Nancy Warren

Nancy Warren

JUST ONE NIGHT

Recycling programs
for this product may
not exist in your area.

ISBN-13: 978-0-373-79710-3

JUST ONE NIGHT

ABOUT THE AUTHOR

USA TODAY bestselling author Nancy Warren lives in the Pacific Northwest where her hobbies include skiing, hiking and snowshoeing. She's an author of more than thirty novels and novellas for Harlequin and has won numerous awards. Visit her website at www.nancywarren.net.

Books by Nancy Warren

To get the inside scoop on Harlequin Blaze and its talented writers, be sure to check out blazeauthors.com.

All backlist available in ebook. Don't miss any of our special offers. Write to us at the following address for information on our newest releases.

Harlequin Reader Service
U.S.: 3010 Walden Ave., P.O. Box 1325, Buffalo, NY 14269
Canadian: P.O. Box 609, Fort Erie, Ont. L2A 5X

To Sally, the best stager I know!

1

"SICK LEAVE?" Rob Klassen yelled, unable to believe what he was hearing from the editor of *World Week,* the international current affairs magazine he'd worked for as a photojournalist for twelve years. "I'm not sick!"

Gary Wallanger pulled off his glasses and tossed them onto his desktop cluttered with Rob's proof sheets documenting a skirmish in a small town near the Ras Ajdir border between Tunisia and Libya. "What do you suggest I call it? Shot-in-the-ass leave? You damned near got yourself killed. Again."

Gary didn't like his people getting too close to the action they were reporting on and his glare was fierce.

Rob put all his weight on his good leg, but even so, the throbbing in his left thigh was hard to ignore. "I was running away as fast as I could."

"I saw the hospital report. You were running toward the shooter. Bad luck for you. They can tell those things from the entry and exit wounds." In the uncomfortable silence that followed Rob heard the roar of traffic, honking cabs and sirens on the Manhattan streets far below. He hadn't counted on Gary finding out the details he'd have rather kept to himself.

"You want to be a war hero," his editor snapped, "join the forces. We report news. We don't make it."

Another beat ticked by.

"There were bullets flying everywhere. I got disoriented."

"Bull. You were playing hero again, weren't you?"

Rob could still picture the toddler cowering behind an oil drum. Yeah, his boss would have been happier if he'd left her scared and crying in the line of gunfire. But he was the one who had to wake up every morning and look himself in the mirror. Truth was he hadn't thought at all. He'd merely dashed over to the girl and hauled her to safety. Getting shot hadn't been in his plan.

Would he have acted any differently if he'd known what the outcome would be? He sure as hell hoped not.

He knew better than to tell Gary any of that. "You don't win Pulitzers with a telephoto lens. I needed to get close enough to capture the real story."

"Close enough to take a bullet in the leg."

"That was unfortunate," Rob admitted. "I can still handle a camera though. I can still walk." He made a big show of stalking across the carpeted office, scooting around the obstacle course of stacked back issues, piled newspapers and a leaning tower of reference books. If he concentrated he could manage to stride without a limp or a wince though he could feel sweat begin to break out from the effort.

"No." The single word stopped him in his tracks.

He turned. "I'm the best you've got. You *have* to send me back out on assignment."

"I will. As soon as you can run a mile in six."

"A mile in six minutes? Why so fast?"

Gary's voice was as dry as the North African desert. "So the next time you have to run for your life you can make it."

Rob paused for breath and grabbed a chair back for support. He and Gary had been friends for a long time and he knew the guy was making the right decision even if it did piss him off. "It was pure bad luck. If I'd dodged right instead of left..."

"You know most people would be pretty happy to be alive if they were you. And they'd be thrilled to get a paid vacation." Gary picked up his glasses and settled himself behind his desk.

"They patched me up at the closest military hospital. It was nothing but a flesh wound."

"The bullet nicked your femur. I do know how to read a hospital report."

Damn.

"Go home. Rest up. The world will continue to be full of trouble when you get back." Rob knew Gary was still aggravated by the fact that he didn't compliment him on his photos, which they both knew to be superb. Instead of getting the praise he deserved, he was being sent home like a kid who'd screwed up.

He scowled.

Home.

He'd been on the road so much in the past few years that home was usually wherever he stashed his backpack.

If he'd ever had a home, it was in Fremont, Washington, a suburb of Seattle that prided itself on celebrating counterculture, considering itself the center of the universe and officially endorsing the right to be peculiar. Fremont seemed a fitting destination for him right now that he was feeling both self-centered and peculiar. Besides, it was the only place he could think of to go

even though everything that had made the place home
was now gone.

"All right. But I heal fast. I'll be running six-minute
miles in a couple weeks. Tops."

"You'll be under a doctor's care and I'll be needing
the physician's report before I can reinstate you for any
assignments in the field."

"Oh, come on, Gary. Give me a freakin' break."

Once more the glasses came off and he was regarded
by tired hazel eyes. "I *am* giving you a break. I could
assign you to a desk right here in New York. That's
your other option."

He shook his head. No way he was being trapped in
a small space. He didn't like feeling trapped. Not ever.
"See you in a couple of weeks."

Once he was out of Gary's office and in the hallway Rob gave up the manly act and tried to put as little
weight on his injured leg as possible.

"Rob, you should be on crutches," a female voice
called out.

He turned, recognizing the voice and mustering a
happy-to-see-you smile. "Romona, hi."

A print business reporter making the transition to
television, Romona had the looks of a South American
runway model and the brains of Hillary Clinton. They
got together whenever they were both in New York.
Neither had any interest in commitment but enjoyed
each other's company and bodies. "I heard you were
hurt. How are you doing?" she asked.

He shrugged. "Okay."

Even though they'd never do anything as obvious
as hug in public, the glance she sent him from tilted
green eyes steamed around the edges. She dropped her

voice. "Why don't you come over later and I'll kiss you all better?"

"I'm filthy. Haven't shaved in days, had a haircut in weeks, my—"

"I like you scruffy. You look like a sunburned pirate."

He knew he'd hit rock bottom when he realized he had no desire to spend the night with a passionate woman. His leg was burning, he had a vicious case of jet lag and he'd been pulled out of the field. He felt too worn-out tired even to get laid. All he wanted to do was hide out for a while and heal.

He shook his head attempting to appear more disappointed than he was. "Sorry. I have a plane to catch."

She knew as well as he did that plane tickets could be changed and it was a measure of his exhaustion that this was the best excuse he could come up with.

She didn't call him on it though, merely patted his arm and said, "Maybe next time."

That was the great thing about Romona. She was a lot like him. He'd enjoyed any number of women over the years, loved sex, but had no interest in settling down. Career came first. Maybe it was shallow, and maybe there was a part of him that longed for a woman to comfort him, to listen to his stories, share his pain. The only woman who'd ever been like that, though, had been his grandmother. Ruefully, he suspected she'd been the love of his life.

And now she was gone.

He had so many frequent flyer miles that upgrading was no problem when he got to LaGuardia. He even scored an aisle seat so he could stretch his bad leg out a little.

Once airborne, he recalled that the family attorney

had tried to talk to him about the Fremont house. What with getting shot and all, he hadn't got around to calling back. He'd call him as soon as he got into Seattle.

It was something to do with Bellamy House, the old family place where he'd spent so much time with his grandmother.

He couldn't imagine the place without her. As a stab of pain hit, he took out the paperback he'd brought and forced himself to read.

HAILEY FLEMING WAS a woman with an agenda. Two in fact. The electronic one that she relied on so heavily that she'd recently started keeping a backup paper day planner because the thought of somehow losing her electronic schedule made her feel too close to losing her mind for comfort.

She was nothing if not organized.

And both agendas told her that she was exactly on time for the best appointment of the day. An after-work glass of wine with a colleague who'd become a close friend, Julia Atkinson.

As she made her way into the bistro off North Phinney Avenue, a former record store turned trendy bar, she scanned the tables and was not surprised to find she was the first to arrive. She was always early.

And Julia was always late.

She settled at a table and ordered a glass of white wine then spent ten minutes going through tomorrow's appointments and writing some notes on improvements she wanted to make on her website.

"Am I late?" a breezy, breathless voice said as Julia swished into her chair, a loose black garment that resembled a combination sweater, poncho and cloak settling in around her.

"Of course you are. You're always late."

Julia's red hair was newly cut into a curly bob and her full lips curved in a smile. "I was at the opening of a new furniture gallery which has brought in several fantastic new lines from Milan. I got chatting, and there were these delicious cookies. I left after three. It was the only way I could stop myself. I don't feel guilty. I bet you did a day's work while you waited."

"Half a day's anyway."

A waiter arrived and Julia ordered a vodka tonic. Which meant she was on another of her diets. Which meant…

"I think I've met someone." She sounded so excited that Hailey leaned forward.

"Tell me everything."

Julia unbuttoned the cloak thing and draped it over the back of her chair, revealing a black-and-red dress enlivened by one of the hundreds of chunky, glitzy vintage necklaces she owned.

"He's an engineer who lives downtown. He was married, but his wife left him and broke his heart."

"Wow. That was fast. I just saw you last week. Where did you meet him?"

Julia's drink came and she took a quick sip. "I haven't actually met him yet."

"Huh?"

She shrugged, and the slight movement made all the rhinestones in her jewelry glitter under the bar's chandeliers. "I met him on LoveMatch.com."

"Oh. Online dating."

"I'd never tried it before, but lots of women meet great guys online. So I figured, why not? It's not like you meet men if you're a home stager." She thought for a second. "At least not straight men."

"How do you already know so much about him?"

"We've been talking on the phone. He's away on business in the Philippines, but I'll be meeting him next Tuesday." Her eyes were bright with excitement. "Do you want to see a picture?"

"Of course."

Julia hauled her computer tablet out of her bag and within a few moments passed over the electronic device complete with a grinning blond guy. Not Hailey's type at all. Too pretty for her tastes, but Julia liked her men pretty. "Wow."

"My big fear is that he's too good-looking for me. Oh, and he has the cutest accent. He was born in Manchester, but he's lived all over the world. An army brat like you."

Hailey regarded the electronic image once more. He was wearing shorts and a loose cotton shirt. Despite the square jaw, he seemed somehow lacking in character. She'd never say so to her friend. Besides, even she knew that her own taste was notoriously picky.

"He's not too good-looking for you. You are beautiful."

"Do you think I can lose ten pounds by Tuesday?"

"Stop it," Hailey said, trying not to laugh. "He's seen your photo, right? He obviously liked what he saw."

Julia nibbled her lower lip. "I used one from after I took that fitness boot camp last year. When I was thinner."

For a smart, self-confident woman, Julia had body-image issues and Hailey knew there was no point arguing. Instead she went with a reassuring "It will be fine."

"I guess. I just have such terrible luck with men." Julia took a last, longing glance at the picture and then put the tablet away. "How are you?"

Hailey let the excitement she'd been feeling all day bubble out. "I have news, too."

Julia's eyes bugged out. "You met a guy?"

"No. I don't have time for men. I'm building a business. Once I feel more successful, then maybe in a couple of years…"

"I know. You and your agendas."

"Lists keep me on track." She sometimes thought she'd had so much chaos in her life that relying on lists gave her a sense of control and stability that she'd never had growing up. Moving twelve times in thirteen years when she was a kid had given her a need for order. Her poor mother had quit even trying to decorate their homes. What was the point? So home had always been temporary and she'd grown to hate the sight of a moving box.

She didn't need psychoanalysis to understand why she'd chosen a career in real estate. She loved helping clients buy permanent homes. The kinds of places where you could plant a sapling and know you'd be around to enjoy the shade of the tree.

"Don't you miss having a man in your life?" Julia lowered her voice. "Don't you miss sex?"

"I have lots of men in my life. Realtors, clients, friends."

One of Julia's eyebrows went up. "And sex?"

"I have sex." Even to her ears she sounded defensive. "Okay, not a lot of sex. It's been a while, but sex for me means commitment. I can't do casual." She shrugged. "Ever since my engagement ended…" She'd believed Drake, who was a lawyer, was perfect for her. They'd worked together on a few closings. They were both hard-working and ambitious. It wasn't until they were talking wedding dates that they'd realized how little their agendas meshed. He wanted to move to New York to a bigger firm. She was building a business in Seattle. He wanted children right away. She felt they should wait a couple of years until the marriage had strong roots. A year ago he'd gone to New York without her. Since then she'd thrown herself into work and hadn't missed Drake as much as she would have imagined.

"He was a moron to pick New York over you."

"Thank you. I agree!"

"So, your big news?"

"I got an amazing listing today. It's my big break. Uncle Ned, an old friend of my father's, called me out of the blue and offered me the Bellamy House."

Julia's eyes widened once more. "That beautiful old place on the hill?"

"Yeah. The woman who owned it died a couple of months ago. Uncle Ned is her executor. There's a grandson and he okayed the sale."

"That's terrific."

"I know." She turned mock serious. "There's just one problem."

Julia grabbed her hand. "It needs staging?"

"Yes! The problem is I need it staged right away. I think I have the perfect buyers. I hate to ask you, but do you think you could stage it tomorrow? I'd love to show them the place Thursday morning."

"Miracles are what I do." Julia morphed from love-addicted friend into professional home stager, tapping at her tablet, then nodding. "Do you have the key to the place?"

"Yes."

"If you can show me the home tonight, I'll figure

out what I need and by tomorrow night, you'll have your miracle."

"I can't wait to show you. This house is going to change everything for us."

2

ROB'S BACKPACK WEIGHED a thousand tons as he hauled it out of the back of the cab. His eyes were dry and gritty and his leg hurt like a son of a bitch. Fog had grounded the plane in Chicago turning a relatively straightforward eight-hour trip into a two-day ordeal. He'd never yet figured out how to sleep on airplanes. Not a real plus for somebody whose job required constant travel.

But he was finally home. Or as close to a home as anything he'd ever known.

As he stood gazing at the big old house, a pang of sadness hit him that was as vicious and intense as his bullet wound.

His grandmother was gone.

He hadn't even made it home for her funeral, her death had occurred so quickly. Not that she'd have wanted him there, but he'd have liked to have been for his own sake. They'd seen each other a few months back when he'd come to visit between assignments. Had she seemed more frail?

Worse, had she known her end was near and not told him?

He shook his head. No.

At eighty-eight his grandmother had impressed him as being mentally as sharp as ever. She'd even chided him to hurry up and get married and give her some great-grandbabies before she got to a hundred. Naturally he'd told her the truth. That he'd never settle until he found somebody like her. Hadn't happened in thirty-five years. He doubted it ever would.

She'd laughed and told him he'd have to set his sights lower. He grinned at the memory. No. His grandmother definitely hadn't planned on dying.

Damn it. He was going to miss that woman.

There were affairs to settle and likely some papers to sign. Right now though all he could think about was a huge glass of Pacific Northwest water, the kind you could drink straight from the tap, a long, hot shower, and sleep.

Long, uninterrupted sleep in a real bed.

As Rob hefted his pack and limped up the path he noted that somebody had swept the front steps recently and even planted blooming bushes in the brick planters.

For early September the night was cool, but to a man who'd spent the past few weeks in the African desert, almost everywhere seemed cool.

He couldn't imagine who would have planted bushes, or why. His brain was way too tired to puzzle out such minor mysteries. Tomorrow. He'd think tomorrow.

As a Realtor, Hailey liked to think of herself as a matchmaker putting the right house together with the right buyer. As of today she had a new unattached single waiting for the right person to fall in love with it—a loft condo downtown that she'd listed this morning, thanks to a referral from a satisfied client. She was new enough to the business that every referral, every listing and especially every sale filled her with pride.

Now she was ready to make another match.

She had a gut instinct that the Bellamy House she was about to show Samantha and Luke MacDonald was going to be a fit. A real-estate marriage made not in heaven but in the offices of Dalbello and Company, where she worked fiendish hours to make her mark in a competitive business.

Like any good matchmaker, she'd prepped carefully, hiring Julia to stage the faded but solid turn-of-the-century Craftsman and bringing in cleaners and a window washer. Hailey had planted cheerfully blooming winter kale and pansies at the entranceway in an effort to keep the buyers' eyes from going immediately to the neglected garden. She wished she had the time and resources to do more, but this was an estate sale.

Everything was as perfect as she could make it. The sun shining on the gleaming diamond-paned windows showed the gracious contours of the home that must have been a real showpiece in its day.

The young couple scheduled to see the place arrived at eleven as scheduled. "I think you're really going to like this one," Hailey said, passing them a feature sheet. "It's just come on the market and I immediately thought of you."

She unlocked the shiny black front door and light spilled into the foyer bringing out the gleam on the newly waxed oak floors. It was amazing what a good cleaning could do to a house. Not that the previous owner hadn't been a good housekeeper; Hailey could tell from the order in the home that she had. Still, in the months since Agnes Neeson had died, the house had been shut up and grown dusty. Today the air smelled not of must as it had the first time she'd viewed it, but of the lilies and roses that Julia had placed in a glass vase on the entranceway table.

Her heels clacked on the original hardwood floors as she pointed out the spacious dimensions of the dining and living areas, the original heritage features such as the hand-carved fireplace mantel and the built-in glass-fronted cabinets. Julia had indeed worked a miracle, hauling clutter and the dated furniture to a storage facility and replacing it all with modern pieces and splashes of designer color in cushions and throws.

She could tell Samantha and Luke were excited and she shared a little of the thrill. Who wouldn't want a great house like this? It was barely in their price range but she knew they could do it. She glanced over at the couple, arguing good-naturedly about where they'd put his wine fridge and how hard it would be to baby-proof the place.

"You could put in a new kitchen, the space is here," she said as she walked them through it. Personally she liked the big old cupboards and the cheerful yellow walls. She suspected though that the MacDonalds would probably prefer stainless appliances and granite countertops. When Samantha reminded her husband that they'd have to build renovation costs into their budget she knew she'd guessed right. He groaned theatrically, but his grin indicated he was excited about the home, too.

Hailey loved being single in the city. All the same there were times, like now, when she got a glimpse of another life. A man at her side, a baby on the way—and a home.

She loved the way Julia had artfully tossed a purple

woolen throw over a gray couch to give the impression that someone with great taste and no clutter lived here.

"Four bedrooms?" Samantha asked.

"That's right. One's ideal for the baby's room, there's a nice-sized room for a guest bedroom, a home office, and the master is a treat. Come on, I'll show you."

They reached the top landing. She first showed them the two smaller rooms and the main bathroom, fine but nothing special. Then she opened the door to the master. "This is my favorite room in the house. There's a vintage four-poster that you might be able to buy with the house if you're interested. It's a large room with wonderful dimensions, a window seat, a fireplace and a full en suite." She flipped on the overhead light. She knew the room by heart but wanted to watch their faces when they saw the blissful space.

Hailey ushered them into the room. "What do you think?"

She was so ready for squeals of delight that Sam's reaction was puzzling. The woman's eyes opened wide. She blinked, looking over at her equally stupefied husband.

Hailey turned around and saw that the white bedcover she'd so carefully smoothed to rid it of any wrinkles was marred, not by a wrinkle, but by a big unshaven man in a blue-and-green checked work shirt, worn jeans and socks that didn't match.

He was sound asleep.

Two grubby sneakers sat on the Aubusson rug where he'd obviously kicked them off prior to napping.

Silence reigned for a moment.

"Does *he* come with the place?" Samantha asked.

Sleepy blue eyes blinked at them out of a lean, weathered, stubbly face. The stranger's overgrown brown hair was more tangle than style. He regarded them, seeming to consider the question, and cracked a smile. "Everything's negotiable." His voice was low, a little husky from sleep.

Sam giggled, thank heaven, though Hailey didn't find anything amusing about finding a homeless guy with a whacked sense of humor snoozing in the house she was trying to sell.

His gaze then focused only on her and she felt the strangest sense of connection with this utter stranger. For a second their gazes held, her heart sped up and she felt as though something that had been out of place suddenly had clicked back in. She closed her eyes against the strange sensation.

She tried to ask "Who are you?" and "What are you doing here?" but in the rush to get it all out her brain short-circuited and instead she asked, "Who are you doing here?"

The twinkle in his blue eyes deepened and when he smiled she noted he had Bradley Cooper–white teeth. No homeless guy she'd ever seen had teeth that gleaming. "I'm not doing anybody here."

Sam giggled again as if they were at an impromptu comedy club.

"I meant what are you doing here?"

He yawned and settled himself onto his back. "Until you showed up I was sleeping."

You didn't get to be a top Realtor—okay, an up-and-coming Realtor—without a lot of tact, so she didn't take off her shoe and throw it at his head, as much as she was tempted. "Okay, let's try the other question. Who are you?" she asked, in a calm, clear voice.

"Robert Klassen. And you are?"

"My name is Hailey Fleming. I'm a Realtor and this house is for sale."

He put up two hands with nails that could use a scrub and rubbed his eyes. "Is that why the place looks like a furniture store? I barely recognized it. My grandmother sure never had such modern taste. The only thing I recognize is this bed." He glanced at the MacDonalds. "She died in it."

Sam made a startled sound, and took a step back, glancing around as though a ghost might be hovering in the room.

Hailey's sale fell through in that moment. She knew it as well as she knew that if she had her way that bed would see another casualty very soon.

"She didn't die here in the house," Hailey said through gritted teeth. "She passed away peacefully in hospital." She doubted the MacDonalds would believe her. For some reason they believed this guy. Was he really Mrs. Neeson's grandson? If he was, she had to tread carefully.

The house bore no signs of a break-in and the scruffy backpack leaning against the wall shouted Drifter. However, a pretty fancy camera bag leaned beside it. Hadn't she heard the grandson was some kind of photographer?

Her unwanted visitor didn't leap off the bed and race for the door, rather he simply grabbed hold of the two green silk accent pillows behind him and propped himself up. Even wearing mismatched socks, he was imposing, undeniably gorgeous in that annoying unkempt way that only certain men can pull off.

She had absolutely no idea how to proceed. Not that she had years of experience under her belt, but she doubted a scenario like this happened very often to any agent, no matter how experienced. And she really,

really needed to keep this listing. It was her biggest break yet in an industry that was tough to crack. The estate lawyer was an old family friend giving her a chance. For some shaggy backpacker to come in here and take it away from her was too much.

However, until she got this mess sorted out there wasn't much she could do, so she pulled herself together and turned to the MacDonalds. "I am so sorry. There is obviously some kind of a mix-up that I will have to sort out before we go any further."

"We understand," said Luke. He stepped back out into the hall. "It's too bad though. It's a great house. Perfect for our needs."

"I know." At least she had the satisfaction of knowing she'd been correct about the match. Thanks to tall, dark and shaggy, it wouldn't fatten her bank account, but at least she knew she was on the right track. "I promise to get things figured out, and when I do, you'll be the first people I call. In the meantime I'll put together some more houses that will work for you."

As they went down the stairs, Sam glanced back over her shoulder. "Did the previous owner really die in this house?"

"Of course not. If she had I'd tell you. Agnes Neeson died in hospital. She was almost ninety and lived here happily until a few days before she passed on. It was a stroke. She died peacefully without ever regaining consciousness. We should all be so lucky."

She kept her bright smile intact until she'd seen the MacDonalds out and then she dropped the happy act and turned back to confront the complete stranger who was doing his best to upset all her careful plans.

Hailey had no intention of letting that happen and tall, dark and disheveled was about to find that out.

3

Rob yawned and stretched, wanting to close his eyes and finish that long sleep he so desperately needed. He heard the front door slam and groaned; clearly he wasn't alone in the house.

With ominous certainty he knew the woman who had so rudely woken him was on her way back to the bedroom. And he didn't think she was going anywhere anytime soon.

He listened as she marched up the stairs, striking the creaky section in the middle of the sixth step. There was another creaky spot on step eleven and she struck that one, too.

This house had no secrets from him.

When she appeared in the doorway of the bedroom he was ready for her. Not at so much of a disadvantage.

Of course, his grandmother would have been horrified to see him lounging on the bed, leaning against stacked pillows he didn't recognize any more than anything else in this room.

He felt almost as though he were in a dream where things were familiar but weren't. The woman currently surveying him was real though. No question there.

She was also hot, he realized, surveying her. She looked pissed off yet confused and unsure of herself all at once. An interesting combination.

He liked the neat way she'd put herself together. She had long blond hair and eyes that couldn't make up their mind between gray and blue and so made you keep noticing them, to wonder.

She wore a black skirt and white blouse with chunky black jewelry. She had nice legs. She might have a nice smile; however, at the moment her lips were so tight together they could be sewed shut.

Then she opened them. Not to smile unfortunately. To speak.

"We have to talk."

He let his head fall back, and if it weren't for all the fancy pillows on the bed he'd have hit the walnut headboard. "Four most frightening words in the English language."

He almost got a glimpse of her smile, but to his consternation she managed to suppress it. "I think there's been some kind of mistake."

"Yeah. I think so, too." He glanced around the room once more. "Did you move in here or something?"

"Of course not. I told you, I'm a Realtor. I've listed this house for sale."

"Well, unless my grandmother spent the last months of her life redecorating her house in condo-modern, somebody else's stuff is in here."

She looked at him as though he was missing half his marbles. He was tired, but he couldn't be that tired.

"I had this home professionally staged."

When it was clear he didn't have a clue what she was talking about, she continued.

"We clear out the clutter and bring in pieces and accessories to showcase the home in the best way possible. I think the improvement is amazing."

"It doesn't look like my grandmother's house anymore." Except for the big bed which he'd instinctively been drawn to last night. It had reminded him of home, tradition, his grandmother.

As he stared up at her, suddenly the four-poster filled him with other thoughts. Adult thoughts. Her slim hands wrapped around the bedposts while she writhed in passion. He blinked, glancing away before she could catch the lust in his eyes.

"It's not supposed to. The concept of staging is to inspire the buyer to see the possibilities and leave them space to imagine their own furniture and personal items in the home."

There were all sorts of things he could reply, such as, he wanted his grandmother's stuff brought back. Even as tired as he was, still he knew that what he really wanted was his grandmother back and that wasn't going to happen. So he went on the offensive. "You need to move all this crap out of here."

Her eyes shifted more to gray when she got huffy. She crossed her arms in front of her. "I have a listing agreement."

"Not with me."

"My agreement is with Mrs. Neeson's attorney."

"That's a funny thing, because the house was left to me." He had to be honest though. "I do remember some weird-ass conversation with her lawyer. I was in Libya with a camp of rebels. It was a bad connection. Maybe he thought I said yes to listing the house when I didn't." He scrubbed his hands across his eyes. He'd kill for a cup of coffee. "I'll probably sell, but I haven't figured out what I'm going to do yet."

"This puts me in a very difficult position." She seemed not to know what to do. He got the impression that she was as staged as the house she was attempting to sell. All at once it occurred to him that she was pretty new at this biz. Probably hadn't come across any difficult situations yet.

Well, she was in one now.

A frown marred her pretty face. "I don't want to be rude but I have no proof you are Mrs. Neeson's grandson.

He figured she had a point, and he already sensed she was stubborn enough that she wouldn't leave until she was satisfied he was who he said he was. So he shifted until he could reach his wallet, took it out, seeing it through her eyes as a grubby, falling-apart-at-the-seams excuse for a wallet. He opened the Velcro flap that was only half stuck down and offered her his driver's license.

She took a look. Stared at him and back at the picture as if she was a bouncer wondering if his ID was fake. "You don't have the same last name."

"That's right. It's a maternal/paternal thing."

"I think maybe you should leave and we'll sort this out tomorrow."

He was no more going to leave this house than he was going to put up with being bossed around by an uppity blond in too-high heels. "That's not going to happen." Enough already. He wanted to get back to his nap. In peace. "Let's call Edward Barnes. He knows me."

"He's on a wine-tasting trip in California. And if you actually know him, you'll know he—"

"Doesn't carry a cell phone," he finished for her, feeling increasingly irritated. He prided himself on keeping cool in a crisis but this was getting ridiculous. "How did I get in?"

She looked at him, puzzled.

"I opened the door, which was locked. How did I get in if I'm not her grandson?"

"The key hidden under the planter. Probably the second place anyone would look, after checking under the mat."

"I am not leaving here. I am the legal owner of this home."

"All I'm asking you to do is prove it."

He jumped up as the obvious solution struck him. "Photo albums with pictures of me and my grandmother."

She looked guilty. "Remember what I told you about decluttering?"

"Where are the photo albums?"

"In storage."

This was turning into a bad farce. You might as well try and milk a rhinoceros as reason with this woman. Some of the old neighbors might have recognized him but most had moved on. Or died.

It was difficult to think when he was in a bedroom, in a bed, and a very attractive woman was alone with him. In heels. Now he pictured her in nothing but those black heels stretched out on the white expanse of the bed.

He had to get out of here. And soon, before he was as hard as one of the bedposts. He shifted and sat up. "Follow me."

She was instantly suspicious. "Follow you where?"

"My first choice would be to the front door—" he was lying, it was his second choice "—but if that's not going to happen, then I want to show you something in my old bedroom down the hall." He scowled as he maneuvered his legs off the bed, trying not to wince, and headed for the door. "I mean, what used to be my old bedroom. Before you turned it into a nursery." Which was why he'd had to crash in his grandmother's bed instead of his own.

His progress was halting at best. She followed slowly, then said, "Oh, my gosh. We moved a black cane into storage. I assumed it was Mrs. Neeson's. Was it yours?"

"No. It was my grandmother's." He didn't feel like explaining. Especially since she supposedly didn't even believe he was Mrs. Neeson's grandson.

"Oh, good."

She wisely refrained from further comment and simply followed his slow progress to the room that had been his for what seemed like his entire life. His grandmother had let him redecorate it after his parents got divorced and maybe that had helped him feel like there'd always be somewhere in his life that was permanent.

The daylight filtered through the dormer window and he remembered all the mornings he'd lain in bed, gazing at the sky, dreaming of travel, of adventure, of a future where he set his own rules.

Under the dormer was a window seat. He noted that the stager had placed a fancy cushion on top of the spot where he'd folded himself into the space between the walls and read comic books hour after hour.

He removed the designer cushion, tossed it onto the faux-leather chair neither he nor his grandmother would ever have chosen. He pulled up on the wooden top of the box and it gave slightly.

"That doesn't open," she said in a smug tone. "We tried it."

"Yeah it does." He'd worked ages on the project figuring out an intricate puzzle opening to keep his stash

of treasures secret. The cool thing about his grandmother was that she'd never asked him how to get into
the thing. Never asked him what he kept in there. She
was the kind of woman who respected a man's privacy
and trusted him with his secrets. He wished there were
more women like that in the world.

When Hailey moved closer to check out what he was
doing he caught her scent. Elusive, feminine, sexy as a
woman in nothing but stilettos. And maybe a wisp or
two of lingerie.

He slid his index finger into the familiar groove.
His fingers were thicker now he'd grown up but he
could still maneuver the latch that raised the top another inch, allowing him access to the second mecha-
nism. It took him another minute and then he lifted the
lid all the way, staring down into the hollow box for the
first time in years.

There wasn't much there. A few old comics he'd
never part with. He pushed his first baseball glove out
of the way, a dog-eared *National Geographic,* and there,
underneath a wooden knife he'd carved himself in his
Samurai phase, was the leather folder. He took it out,
brushed a dead moth off, and handed it to her. He rose
from his crouched position and looked over her shoulder as she opened it.

Once more he caught her scent. Not flowery. Citrus
with underlying tones of heat.

The photograph and accompanying citation were
among his few treasures. "You won a city-wide pho-
tography contest," she said. "You were in high school."
When she turned to him he was struck again by the
blue-gray eyes. Like her scent, the first impression was
coolness, and then you caught the heat behind the cool
facade.

"Yes, but that's not the point. Check out the picture. And read the caption."

An absurdly young version of himself in a sports jacket—one of half a dozen times in his life he'd ever worn anything formal—his grandmother and his mom stood in a little trio, him holding his winning photograph—a bear cub sitting on top of a Dumpster eating an apple. It wasn't much of a big event in a person's life but to him that award had signaled the beginning of a career. Becoming a photojournalist had given him freedom, adventure, life on the road and a reasonable salary.

She read aloud. "'Robert Klassen, fifteen, wins for his photograph, An Apple a Day, while his mother, Emily Klassen, and his grandmother, Agnes Neeson, look on."

He pointed to his young self. "That's me and that's my grandmother."

Her expression softened in a smile. "It's a great photograph. And you were a very cute teenager." She closed the folder and handed it back to him.

"Are you satisfied now that I am who I say I am?"

She turned her head and he was struck once more by the impact of those in-between-blue-and-gray eyes. "You pretty much had me when you opened the Chinese-puzzle-box window seat."

"I'm sorry about the misunderstanding." He was, too. Apart from being a little high-strung, she seemed like a nice woman. "Thing is, I haven't decided yet whether I'm going to sell the place. And if I do I'll want to choose my own Realtor."

Her nostrils flared at that. "Do you have a relationship with a Realtor in Seattle?"

"Not exactly."

"Well, let me tell you, I am an extremely competent Realtor with excellent references. I think the MacDonalds were a real possibility."

"They seemed freaked out that my grandmother died in her bed."

She slammed her hands to her hips. Perfectly manicured hands, no wedding ring. "She didn't. Your grandmother, as I'm sure you know, passed away in hospital."

A shaft of pain stabbed him. Grief, he supposed. He tried to ignore it. "Not the point. If you'd known my grandmother you'd have wanted her spirit to stay in the house." Maybe that was why he had such a heavy feeling when he thought of other people occupying this place. To him she was still here. "People who are scared of ghosts, they wouldn't be my kind of people or my grandmother's." He knew he was overtired and would soon feel more like his old self; until then though he really had to get a grip. And probably stop talking before he made a fool of himself.

The woman smiled at him. "It's hard to let go when we've loved someone," she said softly.

"Yeah." As trite as her words sound, they were sincere.

"Were you close?"

"Oh, yeah. She pretty much raised me." He couldn't imagine what would have happened to him if he'd been left with his mother. His grandmother had not only raised him; she'd saved him. Given him a chance to make something of his life.

When Hailey looked at him, he felt as though she could see inside him. It was the weirdest feeling and he knew she felt it, too, from how she took an instinctive step back toward the door. It was as if they both became aware at the same moment that they were alone together in a bedroom—even if the spread was covered in little yellow duckies. He could have sworn the temperature zoomed up a few degrees.

"Would you like a cup of coffee?" she asked.

That's when he became convinced she really could read his mind. "I would get on my knees and beg for a cup."

A genuine smile tilted her lips. Finally. "No need to beg. I'll meet you downstairs."

He thought about asking her to bring the coffee up but knew she'd get the wrong impression. Thing was, stairs were the hardest for him to navigate. For some reason, which he could not identify, he didn't want this woman to see him limping. "It's okay," he said. "I'll make some later."

"I'd like a cup anyway. And besides, I do want to talk to you."

HAILEY GAVE HERSELF a pep talk as she prepared coffee. *Stay confident,* she reminded herself as she poured freshly ground beans into a French press. *Be positive.* Luckily she'd stocked up on coffee the day before, even had fresh milk in the refrigerator, so it wasn't long before her favorite scent in the world filled the bright kitchen.

She heard a noise behind her and turned to find Robert Klassen in the kitchen. He was taller than she'd first imagined and upright he was more commanding and definitely more sexy.

"Have a seat," she said brightly, pointing to the oak chairs at the kitchen table that she and Julia had decided to keep.

"Thanks." He seemed to hesitate, then moved forward. Slowly. Stiffly. When he went to sit down, he leaned on the table and lowered himself slowly into a chair.

She turned away, busying herself with coffee so he wouldn't think she was staring.

"Do you take milk and sugar?"

"No. Black."

She brought coffees to the table and sat opposite him. According to her electronic planner she had thirty-five minutes until she had to be at the office for the weekly meeting and pep talk. She was determined to use the time to save her listing.

He sipped coffee. Seemed to savor every drop.

"You like your coffee," she said, somewhat amused.

"When you live the way I do, you don't take things like coffee or a good meal for granted. Even clean water is a luxury." He sipped again, caught her gaze and then said, "I got shot. That's why I'm limping. It's no big deal, but I need to rest up for a few weeks."

"Shot? I thought you were a photographer." She wished she'd listened more closely.

"I'm a photojournalist. I work for *World Week*."

World Week was one of the top news magazines in the country, covering international affairs, finance, politics and the arts. "Wow. That must be fascinating."

"It is. Obviously the nature of my job requires me to cover war zones, famines, devastation both natural and human made. As you can imagine there isn't a Starbucks on every corner."

She sipped her own coffee, for once stopping to enjoy the flavor. How often did she even really taste her morning brew? But, with only thirty-four minutes left, she couldn't waste time savoring coffee. She had work to do.

"Do you have a wife and family?"

The question obviously startled him. He nearly choked on his coffee. "No."

"Are you planning to live in this house?"

She asked it innocently, but he had to know where this was going.

A crease formed between his eyebrows. She could see that he was actually thinking about her question. She decided to help him along. "A house this size might not fit with your lifestyle. I imagine you're not home very much."

"See the thing is—"

He stopped talking when they both heard the front door open and a female voice called, "Can I come in?"

Julia. "Sure. In the kitchen," she called back.

"So the coast is clear." And then Julia walked in, a swish of red cashmere coat and black pants, saw the man sitting there and said, "Oh."

His lips twitched, which made her feel once more that strange sense of connection with him. "Julia, this is Robert Klassen."

"I go by Rob," he said as they shook hands.

"Hi, Rob," she said, and flicked Hailey a glance. "Are you interested in buying Bellamy House?"

"I might be, if I didn't already own it."

In a few seconds Hailey had filled her friend in on the situation. Julia poured herself a coffee and sat down. "It's great that you're here to see Hailey at work. She's fantastic. This place will sell in no time." She turned to Hailey. "How did the MacDonalds like it? I think we were genius to stage the small bedroom as a nursery."

"I think they're interested," Hailey said, keeping her tone carefully neutral.

"They're not the right people for this house," Robert Klassen, call-me-Rob, announced.

Hailey and Julia exchanged glances. The unspoken message being *trouble ahead*.

There was an awkward silence, then Julia broke it. "I dropped by to see if you want me to finish the staging on Tuesday night. I had to rush on the upstairs."

"Don't you have a date Tuesday night?" Hailey had been so excited about the blond guy that she had added a notation to her agenda just so she'd remember to phone and ask how the date had gone.

"No. He had to postpone. His business trip has been extended. He's got to go to Nigeria next week. I'll meet him the week after."

"Oh, too bad."

"Gives me time to lose a couple more pounds before we meet." She turned to Rob. "We connected through LoveMatch.com."

"What kind of work does he do?" Rob asked.

"He's a civil engineer."

Hailey said, "I'm not sure about Tuesday. Can I let you know?"

"Sure." Julia took another quick sip of coffee, and then rose. "Sorry to run, but I've got to write up a staging proposal and head to an old friend's baby shower. And I'm already running late. Nice to meet you, Rob."

"You, too."

"I'll call you," Hailey said.

When her friend had gone, she only had twenty minutes to convince this man to let her keep the listing. She opened her mouth to get back to business when he surprised her.

"So your friend hasn't met that guy?"

"What guy?"

"The one she has the date with?"

"No. Not yet. Why?" He was messing with her careful arguments on why she should keep this listing. And besides, what business was it of his if two people he didn't know had a date?

"Tell her he's probably a scammer."

"What?"

"Nigeria is the scam capital of the world. And something about 'civil engineer' sounds fishy to me."

"How can you be so judgmental? She's talked to him on the phone. I'm sure it's fine."

"Maybe. You spend long enough in the news business, you get an instinct." Between telling prospective buyers ghost stories and trying to kill her friend's happy buzz, she wasn't too sure about his supposed instincts. Apparently he didn't have much of an instinct for dodging bullets. "Just tell her, whatever she does, not to send the guy money."

"All right. Fine." She shifted and glanced at her watch. "Can we talk about us?"

He had the sexiest way of looking at her. She'd known the man all of about an hour and every time he looked at her thoughts she had no business thinking flitted through her mind.

"Us?"

As their gazes connected, she thought maybe Julia had a point. It had been way too long since she had sex if a shaggy drifter who was trying to mess with her career could make her overheated with a mere glance. She crossed her legs. "You know what I meant. The listing."

He leaned back in his chair, savored another sip of coffee. Then he said, "Okay. Here's what I propose. You can keep the listing. I'll be living here so you have to work around me. I don't want open houses. Appointment only. We'll see how it goes."

She was so relieved not to find herself fired before

she'd started that she nodded. "Okay." However, she wasn't a complete fool or a pushover. "I have a condition of my own." And she drilled him with her serious-business-woman look. "No more stories about your grandmother dying in that bed. As I'm sure Mrs. Neeson taught you, if you can't say something nice, don't say anything at all."

4

AFTER THE HOT REALTOR LEFT, Rob drained the rest of the coffee into his mug and began to wander through the house.

She was right, of course. It didn't make any sense for him to keep the place. It was too big, with maintenance issues always cropping up. It was a house meant for a family, and now that his grandmother was gone, he didn't have one anymore.

Maybe he hadn't been able to say goodbye formally at her funeral, but he could for damn sure make certain that the next people who lived in this house were a family his grandmother would have approved of.

He suddenly realized that was what had brought him back to Seattle.

He needed to hand on the house to the right people. Then maybe he could let his memories go and get back to his regular life.

If he owed anything to Agnes Neeson's memory it was not to let weenies who were scared of their own shadows live in her place.

He didn't have much of an idea what he was going to do with himself for the next several weeks, apart from get his strength back, so he called Dr. Greene's office and wasn't remotely surprised to get an appointment that very afternoon.

HAILEY BARELY MADE the weekly office meeting at Dalbello and Company, sliding in as the office manager was in the midst of his weekly speech. Normally she worked from home, not interested in renting an overpriced desk. She dropped by to use the photocopy machine and to visit with her mentor and friend, Hal Wilson, who'd been in the business for thirty years.

She saw Hal standing near the water cooler and went over to him. "Did I miss anything?" she whispered.

"Ted says listings are up overall in the city and the house prices are starting to creep up."

"Good news." There were about thirty Realtors in the open area where they held the weekly meetings. Rows of desks stretched out behind her all currently empty. Two high-end printers and photocopiers sat to the side underneath a line of windows. A big whiteboard dominated this end of the room.

Ted told a couple of jokes, gave them a weekly sales tip, and then moved on to the reason she had raced to get here.

"Let's look at the new listings."

He boomed out the listings like an auctioneer. The standard mix of houses, condos, a couple of commercial properties. "And Bellamy House. Listed by Hailey Fleming. Her biggest listing yet and the biggest listing for our office this week." He turned to her with a big two-thumbs-up. "Way to go, Hailey!" He started clapping and all the assembled Realtors joined in.

Sure it was cheesy, but the clapping and cheering worked to make her feel more confident.

Naturally she didn't bother sharing with a group of sharks, all of whom would love to list and sell Bellamy House, that her listing was hanging by a thread.

When the meeting was over, a stylish redhead walked over to Hailey and Hal. "Congratulations again." Her name was Diane and her congrats were as fake as her smile. She was a successful Realtor with a reputation for ruthlessness. "When's the agents' open?"

She shook her head. "The client's very clear. He doesn't want any opens. I've got photos on my website. Give me a call if you've got clients who might be interested. We'll arrange a private showing."

"Will do." Diane asked a couple of questions about the kitchen and made a few notes, then walked off when her cell phone buzzed.

When Diane was out of earshot, Hal said, "I heard she tried to get that listing. She has a contact in the hospital. If a property owner dies, she hears about it before next of kin."

"No!"

He shrugged. "I wouldn't put it past her."

Good thing the lawyer was a family friend. "Hal, I've got a problem. I need some advice."

"Okay."

She told Hal about Rob and the tentative agreement they had that she could keep the listing as long as she didn't disturb him. "I'm sure the MacDonalds would have made an offer if he hadn't scared them off with stories of his grandmother dying upstairs in the bedroom."

Hal took his time answering her, finally, saying, "This is a great opportunity for you. I don't want you to lose it."

"Me neither."

"Some clients don't even know what they want. Sounds like he's one. You're going to have to manage him."

"Manage him? How?"

"Hailey, my dear. Use one of your greatest assets. Your charm."

DR. GREENE'S OFFICE smelled the same as it had for the thirty years he'd been dragged here, Rob thought, as he sat leafing through an ancient golf magazine. And the decor hadn't changed since he was a kid either, he realized as he shifted on the cracked vinyl seat in the waiting room. He tossed the magazine aside. He didn't even like golf. He took out his phone and checked his email. Nothing interesting.

He hated waiting rooms. Hated anything with the word *waiting* in it. He checked the time on his phone. He'd been here fifteen minutes. It wasn't even his idea to be under a doctor's care. Damn Gary and his officious dictates. So his leg hurt. It would heal.

A mom and her kid emerged from the treatment room. The kid hunch-shouldered and coughing. This family doctor was so old-fashioned he only had one room. As soon as the outer door closed behind the cougher and his mom, the receptionist, Carol, who'd been sitting behind that old oak counter since before Rob was born nodded toward him. "You can go on in."

Horace Greene had to be closing in on seventy. His hair, what was left of it, was salt-and-pepper, his beard was Santa Claus–white and his pale blue eyes focused as keenly as ever from behind bifocal lenses. Doc Greene had been his grandmother's family doctor longer than he'd been alive, and if he had a family doctor, he supposed it was this one. Doc rose to his feet as Rob limped into his office and held out a hand.

"Rob, how you doing?"

"Been better, Doc."

The physician gestured to the oak chair in front of his scarred oak desk and took his own seat on the other side. "Haven't seen you in a long time. How long's it been?"

"Must be five years."

He nodded. He might be chitchatting, but Rob wasn't fooled. Those old eyes didn't miss a thing. "Sorry about your grandmother passing. It was a big loss for you."

"Yeah."

"And what's this? You're limping. What happened?"

"I got shot."

If Doc was surprised by the news he didn't show it. "Mmm-hmm, so when was this? Who's looked at it?" He pulled out a notepad and began scribbling.

"About a week ago. On assignment in Libya. My boss pulled some strings and got me in to a military surgeon. He took some X-rays, said there were no remaining fragments. Gave me a few stitches and told me I was good to go."

Doc glanced at him over his glasses and said, "I bet he or she also told you to use crutches."

The military surgeon had said that and a few other less complimentary things. He shrugged. "You know what a fast healer I am. You've always said I've got a head like a rock."

"But you're not bullet-proof. I should take a look at the wound."

"I'm going to need a report from you that says I'm cleared to go back to work."

Doc Greene rose and headed for his treatment room

adjoining the office. "Drop your duds and let's have a look."

Rob followed him, trying his hardest not to limp, and soon found himself sitting on the exam table, his pants folded over a chair, his leg bared to the doctor's prying gaze. And fingers. "Ow."

"No discharge on the bandage and the wound is healing nicely." Doc nodded, tossing the old bandage into the trash. "You said it's been a week since the injury. We'll redress that for you and it should be okay."

The older man fussed around in a cabinet, taking out the things he'd need. "I'm putting on a dry dressing," he said as he began. "Dry gauze and tape. As soon as the wound stops weeping you can leave it open to the air to speed healing. That should happen in the next few days. Pat dry after showers."

"Great, thanks," Rob said after the new dressing was taped to his leg. He was happy he'd got off without a lecture on being careful or some other impertinence from the man who'd been doctoring him for three decades.

But he didn't get off that easy.

"Put your pants back on and come on back to my office. There's a few things I'd like to talk to you about."

Reluctantly, Rob returned to the chair in front of the desk and slumped down.

Doc Greene pushed the pad aside and looked at him intently. "How are you coping?"

"Fine."

A beat of silence passed but Rob wasn't going to break it. Doc continued. "You've been through an emotionally exhausting time. You've lost someone special and you've got a significant enough injury that it's brought you home. All that combined is going to take a toll."

"I'm fine," he repeated, sounding less than fine even to his own ears. This was the man who had treated his grandmother through her few illnesses and had looked after her at the end. He licked his lips. "My grandmother—she seemed fine when I was home six months ago..." He let the unspoken question hover.

Doc sat back. No wonder patients were always kept waiting. He never rushed.

"Agnes Neeson lived a life anyone would be proud of. She kept her independence to the end." Doc smiled. "And you know how important that was to her. She was getting frail. She had a massive stroke and died in hospital without ever regaining consciousness." He didn't need to consult a file. He knew all his patients and he and Agnes had been friends as well as doctor and patient.

"Would she have suffered?"

Doc shook his head. "There are no nerve endings in your brain. There wouldn't be pain."

"Good," Rob said, relieved and somehow comforted. "I wish I'd been there."

Doc nodded. "I know. Reading every issue of *World Week* cover to cover made your grandmother feel close to you. Nobody could have been prouder of you than she was."

The prickling of tears horrified Rob. He cleared his throat and changed the subject fast. "There's a Realtor who messed up the house." He rubbed his sore leg. "She took out my grandmother's furniture and staged the place. Everything's different since I was here."

"It is. I heard the place was for sale. It's that nice young gal from Dalbello who has the listing. She'll do a good job for you."

Rob didn't have the energy to talk about his confused

feelings so he mumbled his thanks and struggled to his feet. Limping to the door, he realized that the doc was right. He wasn't as okay as he tried to pretend he was.

JULIA RAN INTO BEANANZA, her favorite coffee shop. "Hey, Julia. How's it going?" Bruno, her favorite barista, called over the hiss of the espresso machine.

"It's a beautiful day," she called back.

Bruno sent her a disbelieving look out of his big brown Italian eyes. "It's raining," he said. He wore a bill cap, one from his huge collection. She was pretty sure he was sensitive about the thinning patch of hair at the crown of his head, though maybe it was a fashion statement. Who knew?

He had a gold hoop in one ear and wore a T-shirt that said Decaf Is for Sissies.

When he'd served a hot chocolate and a chai latte to the customers in front of her, he started her drink. There was no need to ask, she ordered the same thing every day. A tall skinny latte. As though drinking enough of it might rub off and she'd awaken one day to find herself tall and skinny.

She lived in hope.

While preparing her drink, he said, "Brownies are fresh out of the oven." As though she needed reminding, as though the smell weren't enticing her to sin, leading her down the calorie path of doom. She could see them behind the glass case, the chocolate glistening on top, the cakey part dense and rich. "I can't," she moaned. "I'm on a diet."

"Really? Who is he?"

"Why do you think I'm only on a diet because of a man?"

"Because you've been coming into Beananza nearly

every day for three years. That's like a thousand days in a row. And every time you tell me you're on a diet there's a guy."

"Okay, there's a guy."

He smiled as he passed her latte over. She glanced down at the surface, as she did every morning. And laughed. He'd drawn a heart into the froth on the top of her latte.

She settled into one of the small tables to enjoy her coffee. Bruno always served coffee in china mugs unless a customer specifically asked for a to-go cup. Customers only made that mistake once. Bruno made it very clear he strongly disapproved of people carrying coffees around. He served his brew the way he believed it was meant to be drunk, sitting down and savoring it, and if you didn't like drinking coffee his way, you could go elsewhere.

His café was always packed.

Julia had learned to appreciate Bruno's point of view. She looked forward to settling into one of the small tables or the long bar by the windows. She would sip her coffee and read the paper or a magazine, or, as now, open her tablet computer to savor the latest email from her LoveMatch.

Hi sweetie,

She absolutely loved that he called her *sweetie*. It seemed so casually intimate. As though they'd been a couple for years.

The weather is hot and sticky here. I have to catch a plane soon. We'll be looking at large pipes for a construction project. I miss you so much. I have

never felt so close to someone before. I long to see
you next week.
Love, Gregory

Not only coffee was meant to be savored, she thought
as she read the message again, slowly. Love was meant
to be savored, too. She only hoped Gregory wasn't disappointed when they met in person.

She sent a worried glance down at her latte. Should
she switch to green tea?

ROB LEFT THE DOCTOR'S OFFICE with an aching thigh from
where the good doc had prodded and poked at him. He
didn't like doctors mostly because he didn't like being
sick or incapacitated.

As he limped along the sidewalk, clutching a
scrawled prescription for painkillers he knew he'd never
fill, he got caught in a downpour of rain. He loved the
rain. After the heat and dry dustiness of the desert, the
cooling water dripping from gray skies should have
made him happy. Instead he felt as though the sky was
suffering a massive outpouring of grief. Irritable, achy
and at a loss for something to do, he just stood getting wet.

He didn't want to go back to Bellamy House with all
that designer stuff he didn't recognize, and he didn't
want to visit the few friends he still had in the area. He
wanted to get on a plane and get back to work. That
wasn't about to happen, though, until he could run a
mile in six. He set his jaw, knowing he'd have to walk
before he could run and not for the first time cursed the
trigger-happy rebel who'd fired on him. He squinted
up and down the street and saw the sign for a coffee
shop a couple of blocks away. He figured that would

do for a destination. He'd walk a few blocks today, a few more tomorrow, and in a couple of weeks he'd be up to running.

Crutches. As if.

He took a step toward the coffee shop and another one. Two women chattering away beneath umbrellas passed him. As he stepped around them, he stepped into a puddle and felt the cold wetness soak his sock. Yup, he was home.

By the time he'd gone one block he felt as though someone were jabbing hot pokers into his thigh. The remaining block seemed like such a long way he contemplated stopping where he was, sagging onto a bus stop bench and calling a cab. Turning his head toward the road ensured he no longer saw the tempting bus bench. He squinted at the coffee shop and pushed his foot forward. He liked the name of the café. Beananza. He vaguely remembered driving past it last time he'd been home but he'd never been inside.

He imagined how good that coffee was going to taste when he got past the next block, assuming he could get there before the place closed for the night. One foot in front of the other, he reminded himself. It was only pain, he could get through it.

A car slowed beside him and he paid no attention until the window closest to him slid down and a voice said, "Rob, I found you."

He turned to see Hailey behind the wheel of a small gray SUV, looking as perky as ever in a blue raincoat. "Why were you looking for me?"

She pulled over and parked because it was that kind of a neighborhood—parking spaces were plentiful. She got out, popped a blue umbrella and then reached into the back of her car and took out his grandmother's walking cane.

For a second Rob experienced a pang of grief so sharp it numbed the pain in his leg. That cane had been supporting his grandmother for years. Of course she'd resisted the thing like crazy and then had come to rely on it in her later years.

Hailey came around the back of the car and offered him the worn black handle. "Here."

He wrapped his hand around the handle and tried out the cane. It was a little on the short side but he wasn't going to complain. Strangely, clutching the spot where his grandmother's hand had gripped made him feel better, connected to her in some sentimental fashion that still comforted. "How did you know?"

"Doc called me. He said you could use your grandmother's cane." She seemed a lot warmer than last time he'd seen her. As though she genuinely cared.

"My doctor called you?" His shock must have shown because she laughed. "So much for doctor-patient privilege."

"Your grandmother had quite a network. They all know each other and their business. And their friends' business, and their friends' grandsons' business."

"He told me to go get crutches."

"I know. And he told me you wouldn't. He said to tell you to use the cane on the opposite side to your bad leg."

He switched the cane to the other hand. "Huh."

"Where are you going?" she asked him. "Do you want a ride?"

He shook his head. Under the blue glow from her umbrella, her eyes were as blue as the sky would be if you could see it. "Only tourists use umbrellas," he informed her.

"And people who actually care about their appearance."

"I'm heading for that coffee shop over there," he said, hoping he sounded casual, as though he'd be there in a couple of minutes, no biggie.

"Bruno's place?" she asked.

"Beananza," he said, since he had no idea who Bruno might be.

"Right. That's Bruno's place. I'll come with you." A crease appeared between her perfectly shaped brows. "Or I could drive you."

"It's a block."

"You have a bullet in your leg."

"Do not."

She let out a sigh of frustration. "Whatever."

They started off and he thought he made a pretty respectable showing, thanks to the cane. He hoped his companion couldn't tell how heavily he was leaning on the thing. It was a little awkward, her with her umbrella, him with his cane, as they made their slow way toward the cheerful yellow sign.

To take his mind off the ache in his thigh he checked out her legs, slim and toned and sexy as hell in those heels.

5

AT THE ENTRANCE TO BEANANZA, Hailey shut her umbrella and stepped in front of Rob, pushing the door open so he could limp in without making a big deal of it.

"Since you're a client it's my treat," she said, and he somehow knew she was saving him the hassle of navigating the small tables and trying to balance coffees and the cane. He liked the simple way she helped him without making an issue of it.

"Thanks. An Americano."

"Hi, Hailey," a familiar voice called out.

"Julia." Hailey checked her watch. "I should have known you'd be here." She slipped off her coat and slid it over the back of a wooden chair at Julia's table, pulling out a second chair and angling it so he could slip into it without a lot of maneuvering. "Can I get you another?" She gestured to her friend's half-empty cup.

"No, thanks. I'm counting calories."

While Hailey clacked up to the front, her heels hitting the reclaimed fir floors, he looked around. The place was packed. Two old men at a corner table talked politics; one wore a blazer, as though he'd spent so many years dressing for the office that he couldn't stop even in retirement.

A trio of young mothers gossiped while their off-spring dozed in strollers or gummed some kind of food from a reusable plastic container. A young guy with earphones on typed frantically into a computer. Two Asian women sat in a corner with textbooks and open notebooks.

Change the faces, the clothing and the language, and you could be in any public meeting place in the world, he thought.

"It's funky, isn't it?"

He turned back to Julia. "Yeah. Lots of character. I like it."

"Wait until you taste the coffee. It's so much better than anything you can get in a chain."

He nodded, thinking how people always seem to say that whether it's true or not. "You working?"

"No. Taking an email break." She blushed. "I'm like a teenager. It's ridiculous. He calls me *sweetie*. Isn't that romantic?"

A guy calling a woman *sweetie* might have trouble remembering names, but he kept that thought to himself.

"Have you done much online dating?"

"No. This is my first time. I can't believe I lucked out first time."

Hailey arrived with two steaming china mugs, and placed one down in front of him.

"Thanks."

Hers was some frothy drink. "I got an umbrella," she said to Julia.

He glanced over half expecting that the baristas had taken to putting paper parasols into coffees now.

It would hardly surprise him. Every time he came back to the States there seemed to be some new and crazier innovation—Earl Grey lattes or raspberry flavoring or some damn thing. It turned out though that they were talking latte art. The barista had decorated the foam with the outline of an umbrella. He checked the surface of his own coffee before taking a sip but found it blessedly manly, black and decoration-free.

He drank and found the brew gratifyingly strong.

"I was just telling Rob that my engineer calls me *sweetie* in his emails."

"Oh, that's so cute."

Julia shifted forward in her seat. "I've already lost two pounds. I think I can lose another one before we meet. Do you think I should go for jeans and a sweater for our date? Or do I put on a dress? I can fit into that red one I wore to your birthday last year."

Hailey seemed to ponder the choices the way a judge might consider a felon before a sentencing. "Where are you going on your date?"

"I'm not sure. He asked me which are my favorite restaurants so I assume he wants to go for dinner. He said he's getting his Mercedes tuned up so he can pick me up."

"He drives a Mercedes," Hailey said, sounding impressed.

"Or says he does," Rob mumbled into his coffee. When Hailey moved her chair slightly, he caught her scent again, even over the coffee, or was he imagining that cool citrus underlaid with something hot and dangerous?

"I want to look my best, but I don't want to seem too eager." Julia turned to him. "What do you think? Jeans or dress?"

He wanted to bolt to the other side of the coffee shop and talk politics with the old guys. Instead he tried to recall to the last actual date he'd had. It would be dinner with Romona, after work but before bed. Romona looked hot in jeans, dresses, fancy gowns, and best in nothing at all.

Which didn't seem like information he wanted to share with two women he'd only just met.

"It depends where you're going for the date, I guess. But I like a nice dress on a woman."

Both women listened to him as though he might have the answer to life's greatest mysteries.

"It's more about chemistry than clothing. If you click, you click. It's a bizarre and unpredictable fact of life that sometimes you meet a woman and there's no spark, and sometimes, for no reason at all, there's this huge attraction between you."

Instinctively he glanced at Hailey. The inconvenient attraction was sizzling between them even now, in this crowded coffee shop with steamy windows from all the damp coats and sweaters drying off from the rain. Just the way her body curved into the chair turned him on. The way she held her coffee mug with two hands like a little kid. The way her head tilted when she listened. The sound of her laughter, the shape of her legs. "You have no control, even when it's the last person you want to be attracted to."

Their gazes locked and, as he felt the heat traveling back and forth between them, her lips parted, giving him a glimpse of white teeth and pink tongue.

She blinked and turned away, taking a quick drink from her china mug.

Julia gnawed some of her lipstick off. "I feel a huge

attraction to this guy and I haven't even met him. I can't imagine what will happen when we do meet."

"Neither can I," Rob mumbled.

Hailey reached over and touched her friend's hand while simultaneously kicking him under the table. Luckily his bad leg was on the side farthest from her. "I really hope this works out. He sounds perfect."

As opposed to this huge and inconvenient attraction he felt for Hailey that was far from perfect.

A smart man would keep his distance.

HAILEY RECEIVED A CALL the next morning from Diane, who said she had clients who might be interested in Bellamy House.

Hailey cleared it with Rob and showed up half an hour before Diane and her clients were due, to make sure he was as neat as he claimed he was.

After checking the downstairs rooms and sighing with relief that all she had to do was hide a coat and some boots in the closet and give the kitchen sink a quick polish, she hurried upstairs.

She walked into the master bedroom and discovered Rob had done away with the designer cushions Julia had placed on the bed. She unearthed them from where he'd stuffed them—under the bed.

As she was bending over, fluffing them as close to their original pristine state as she could get them, a voice said behind her, "Are you going to put mints on the pillows and turn down the bed?"

She turned abruptly. "Rob, what are you doing here?" And then her eyes widened. He'd emerged from the master bath in nothing but a towel loosely tied around his hips. His hair was wet, his chest hair clung in damp, dark curls to his skin and one water droplet slid down his shoulder in a way that fascinated her.

He smelled of soap and toothpaste but she could swear she got a whiff of hot, star-filled nights under a desert sky.

"You need to go. I've got a Realtor coming in twenty minutes."

"Her name Diane something?"

How could he know that? "Yes."

"She called here. Her clients couldn't make it today."

"She called here? She should have called me."

He shrugged. "She said she couldn't reach you. We had a good talk on the phone. She knows a lot about this neighborhood. She said she'd be interested in talking to me about the history of the house."

"Oh, did she."

"She also mentioned that you're pretty new in the business, and if I need any advice from a more experienced Realtor she'd be happy to oblige."

Hailey's blood began to boil, but she was determined to maintain her poise. "What did you tell her?" Please let him not have fallen for that phony snake's tactics.

"I told her she should be selling used cars down on Federal Way."

She was so surprised a snort of laughter erupted before she could stop it. "I wish I'd seen her face." She tried not to notice how gorgeous Rob was in nothing but a towel and a few lazy drops of water.

"I don't like those tactics."

"Good."

He took a step closer leaving a damp footprint on the rug. He had narrow feet with long toes. If she concentrated on those she wouldn't obsess about his near-nakedness and the big, tempting bed looming behind them.

"If I dump you for another Realtor it won't be to someone devious."

Her gaze connected with his, warm and intimate. "Are you going to dump me?" Her voice came out husky.

"I don't have you. Yet."

She flashed to an image of herself pushing him onto his back in that bed with one hand while the other rid him of his towel.

The thought was so compelling that she had to clench her fists.

They were inches away and she felt tingly all over. She tried to think of something completely unsexy to say.

"Why were you so negative to Julia about her date?" was the first thing she came up with.

"I wasn't negative," he said. "I told her to wear a dress, didn't I?"

"You sounded sarcastic."

"I have a hard time believing you can fall in love over the internet. The guy sounds like a dick."

"Why? Because he asks her what restaurants she likes? Doesn't drag her to his cave by her hair?"

He reached for his watch on the dresser and she wondered how hard she'd struggle if he tried to drag her to his cave. She suspected not very.

"No. Because he drops into the conversation that his Mercedes needs an oil change. Who does that?"

"He's trying to impress her."

"I think he sounds suspicious."

"You know you're not in a war zone now where every

other person could be a spy or the enemy. You're home. Maybe you should give your suspicion a rest."

He looked as though he wanted to say more. His eyes were a clear green in the morning light. His hair, now almost dry, was trying to curl. "Maybe."

"And maybe they are falling in love on the internet, like old-fashioned pen pals."

He turned to her, his expression intense. "You don't get attracted by words on a computer screen. Sexual attraction is raw and immediate. It's about a man and a woman seeing inside each other." His gaze grew more intense. "It's in the shape of her face, her expression in different lights, the way her hair falls." He reached forward and touched the ends of her hair with his fingertips. As he did so, he brushed her shoulder and she drew in a sudden jerky breath.

She tried to speak and couldn't. He was so close she saw the dark flecks in the depths of his eyes, the freckles on his shoulders.

"It's about the feel of her skin," he said, letting his fingers trace the line of her jaw. Rough fingers that hefted heavy cameras and schlepped equipment through gritty deserts. "The sound of her voice, the way she smells." His voice dropped to a near whisper, its tone deepening. "The way she tastes." And he closed the short distance between them and put his mouth on hers.

Even though she'd anticipated the feel of his kiss, nothing could have prepared her for the lust that punched through her system when their mouths connected. A light, teasing kiss turned hungry and hot in a nanosecond. His hand moved to the back of her head, fisting in her hair, tilting her head so he had better access. She made a little moaning sound in the back of her throat as she reached for him, wanting to feel the solid outline of his chest, to thrust her fingers into his damp hair. He tasted like the cool mint of toothpaste and the hot spice of lust, his tongue teasing and tormenting her, giving and taking in equal measure. She'd never been kissed like this. Never imagined anything close to this.

He kissed her, taking his time, not trying to rip off her clothes or talk her into his bed. He kept kissing her as though his whole existence depended on nothing but this moment.

Getting involved with Rob wasn't on her list or her agenda or anywhere in her short-term plans but she knew in that moment that her careful personal agenda had just been seriously screwed up.

When he drew slowly away from her, gentling his embrace, he grinned at her wryly. "You can't get that on the internet."

She'd have replied except that she was currently speechless.

When he turned to get dressed she scooted out of the room and said softly, "Or anywhere else."

6

JULIA'S HOME PHONE was ringing when she opened the
door to her apartment. She'd left a bridal shower early
to get home since Gregory generally phoned around this
time. It seemed as though all her friends were either getting married or having babies and she wanted that, too.
Excitement bubbled within her when her call display
revealed an international number. "Hello?"

"Hi, sweetie."

"Hi yourself, Gregory. How was your meeting?"

"Long." The line crackled. "I miss you. I miss Seattle. Tell me what's going on?"

"It rained today. Nothing new there. Let's see. I de-
staged a house that sold, no doubt because of my excellent staging."

"Is the statue of Lenin still keeping watch over Fremont?"

She smiled into the phone. "Of course. Oh, and I was
trying to decide what to wear for our date next week. I
can't wait to meet you in person."

"I can't wait either, sweetie. I've never felt so close
to a woman before."

"I know. I feel the same and it's so strange. We've

never even met." She moved a pot of rosemary on her windowsill, centering it. "I noticed you took your profile down."

"I'm not interested in anyone else."

She felt as though she'd endured years of feeling like second-best. Of giving out her number to men who never called her. Of seeing taller, thinner women walk off with guys she was interested in. So to have this man choose her, out of all the women on LoveMatch.com was incredible.

"I feel the same way," she admitted.

They never talked for long, but she always felt like the luckiest woman in the world when she hung up smiling.

She'd booked a hair appointment for Tuesday and then, thinking what the hell, added a mani, pedi and a facial into the mix.

When she imagined that beautiful, sexy man seeing her for the first time, it was easy to make sensible food choices. Dinner was a salad with oil and vinegar and a tasteless piece of broiled fish because she could still lose a pound or two by Tuesday if she remained disciplined.

She was contorted on her green yoga mat, trying to keep up with a Pilates DVD that would tighten her core, define her muscles and—something the cover copy had neglected to mention—make her sweat like a pig, when the ding on her computer signaled an incoming email.

Only too happy to give her core a rest, she leapt up to find, as she had hoped, that the email was from Gregory.

Hi sweetie,
I'm in a jam and I don't know who else to turn to. My ex-wife ran up all my credit cards so I had to cancel

them. My flight was canceled and I need to book a
new one to get home in time for our date. I hate to
ask, but could you wire me the money for the flight?
It will be $1,200. I'll pay you back when I see you.
Love, Gregory.

She read the email a second time, feeling worse by
the second. *Don't jump to conclusions,* she scolded herself. He could be legitimate. Anyone could get stuck
in a foreign country without a credit card. Although it
was hard to imagine why his own company couldn't advance him the money for an airline ticket. In the back-
ground, the Pilates woman was encouraging everyone
to "tighten those glutes as you lift your spine off the
mat. And hold."

Julia sat down in front of the computer, nibbling her
lower lip as she read the email yet again, then began
typing.

Dear Gregory,
I have to admit your request has puzzled me. There
are warnings all over the website about not sending
money to strangers. Maybe if I'd actually met you,
it would be different. How would I even send you
the money?

Within a minute a response came.

Hi sweetie,
Please trust me. I want us to be together.

And then he'd included full instructions on how to
wire money via Western Union.
And that's when she knew she'd been scammed.

"Do NOT SAY, 'I told you so,'" Hailey warned Rob. "Julia's very sensitive about what happened."

He held up his hands. "Hey, I was only trying to warn her. Not trying to score points. I didn't want the guy to turn out to be a scammer. She seems like a nice woman. I'm sorry it happened."

"Okay," she said more mildly.

His eyes crinkled at the edges as he faced her. "But to you, I can say it, right? 'I told you so.'"

"It was the lucky guess of a suspicious mind."

"Bull. It's an instinct honed by years of gathering and reporting news."

"We won't mention her getting scammed when she gets here. I don't want her to feel stupid. It could happen to anyone."

"Why is she coming, anyway?" And Hailey had a feeling there was an unspoken *and why are you here?* in his tone, as well.

Neither of them had mentioned that steamy kiss they'd shared in the bedroom yesterday. She was happy she'd had a dramatic story to impart the minute she got to Bellamy House so there were no awkward silences, no talking about something she preferred to ignore.

Even if Rob did look far too kissable in worn jeans, a much-washed and faded T-shirt advertising some band she'd never heard of and those bare feet that she found ridiculously sexy.

"I'm not happy about the way we've staged the small bedroom upstairs. It was fine to have it as a nursery when the MacDonalds were looking at it. However, most of the people who look won't have a baby so I'm thinking of turning it into an older child's bedroom with a single bed and a desk."

"Can't the people who look at houses figure out where their own stuff will fit?"

She thought about it. "Some can, I guess. Most only see what's in front of them. In this economy we want to do everything we can to make a home so inviting a buyer can't resist. Since this is a family neighborhood with schools nearby and that big park right across the street, it makes sense to stage it for a family."

"So you put a single bed and a desk in it. That's pretty much how it was when I grew up."

"I'm glad you approve of something we're doing. Which reminds me, you're going to have to make yourself scarce. Two sets of potential buyers are coming today between two and three o'clock."

He scowled. "We made a deal. You could keep the listing but I'd be living here."

"And I said I'd work around you. That means you leave fifteen minutes before the appointment time so I have a few minutes to clean up after you."

"Hey, I'm neat."

"I know you are. And what a relief that is, but I'll need to put your shoes away and hide your toothbrush. Stuff like that."

"You leave my toothbrush alone. A man's toothbrush is a personal thing. Handling it implies intimacy."

And just like that the intense lust she'd experienced during that kiss came roaring back. She was trying to forget it, and based on the way he was acting around her, so was he. Now he mentioned intimacy and she felt the warmth of his words touching her.

"Fine. Put away your own toothbrush."

"Okay," he said gruffly and she knew he'd been thinking about that steamy kiss, too.

They heard a knock and then the front door opening. "Hi," called Julia.

"Hi. We're in the kitchen." She put her finger over her lips as a reminder not to mention Julia's troubles.

Julia swept in with all the drama of an opera diva preparing for her final, tragic aria. "I feel so stupid!" she cried. "I am never, ever dating again."

Well, so much for worrying that Rob might bring up a difficult subject. She might have known Julia would be more than happy to share.

Even though her friend spoke in a tragi-comic tone, Hailey could see she'd been crying recently.

She wasn't going to sit by and let a good friend hurt. It was difficult for Hailey to make intimate friendships; she sometimes felt as though she'd never learned how. That's why her friendship with Julia was so important to her.

They'd met at a networking business event and they'd talked a little and laughed a little and exchanged business cards. She was startled when Julia had called her a couple of days later and suggested lunch, but she'd been pleased. They chatted about the industry, about their ambitions and then about men.

She liked Julia's frankness and honesty. Within a couple of weeks they were seeing each other regularly for a yoga class, a drink after work, shopping and brunch. Julia had a big, noisy family who'd lived at the same address for fifty years. She had friends she'd known since kindergarten. She had everything Hailey had never had and always craved.

She watched as Julia, her sisters, brothers and mother would argue, sometimes squabble like kids and then hug and joke minutes later. Julia took her in, made Hailey part of her life. Almost forced her to open up and share.

At some point she realized that Julia was her best friend. Probably the closest woman friend she'd ever had.

And if there was one thing she could do to thank Julia for teaching her what a friend was, it was to be one. So she said, "You are not giving up."

"I knew when I saw the photograph that he was too good-looking for me."

"That wouldn't be his real photo," Rob said. "You know that, right? He's probably a twenty-two-year-old Nigerian kid with a degree who speaks good English. They steal pictures of male models and hope nobody notices."

"I didn't," she moaned. "And I thought his accent was so cute. He said he'd been born in Manchester and moved around a lot. That's why his accent was different." She smacked her forehead with her palm. "And I believed him. I fell for the whole scam, hook, line and sinker."

"No. You didn't," Rob said. "You didn't send any money. So he didn't gain anything." Rob was a lot more direct than Hailey would have been but she could see that his blunt words had an effect. Julia looked slightly less beaten down. While she watched him talking to her friend she realized he was a truly nice guy, and watching his lips move reminded her that he was a great kisser.

And she hadn't been kissed in a long time.

He'd awakened her lusty, sexy side and she didn't think it was going back into hibernation anytime soon. What she was going to do about this, she had no idea.

She wasn't a casual woman and she didn't do casual sex. Still, an image of Rob and her in that big bed upstairs kept intruding. She pictured the two of them, limbs entwined, and a feeling of heat began to spread through her.

"Scammers only win when they get—"

He paused, turned to stare at Hailey, and she felt him sharing her fantasy as surely as if the two of them were naked and entwined at this very moment. The look he gave her was searing, intense. She touched her chest, her fingers resting on her collarbone, and his gaze followed as though he were the one touching her there.

Julia's expression was still bleak. "He gained my trust. I believed the guy. That's what hurts so much. I consider myself an intelligent woman. How could I be so stupid?" She shook her head and her red curls bounced. "Anyway, I'm done with LoveMatch.com."

Julia's pain broke the moment of intense lust and Hailey returned her attention to where it belonged.

"No," Hailey cried. "You can't give up so easily. Then the scam artists really do win. Come on. You're not going to let one bad apple wreck the whole orchard."

"I'm giving up on apples."

"Come on. Get your computer out. We're going to get you a date with a real guy who may not be the love of your life but who exists."

"Wow. How my standards are dropping. I used to think I couldn't date anyone who didn't appreciate Frank Gehry. Now all I ask is that he actually breathes."

Hailey laughed. "It will be fun. You'll feel a lot better once you put this behind you."

"I guess." Julia allowed herself to be persuaded to open her computer and log on to the site. Hailey leaned over her shoulder, watching every keystroke. "What about him?" she asked, pointing when Julia's possible matches appeared.

"I hate beards," she said, and deleted the guy's picture.

"What about him?"

Julia snorted. "The only good thing I can say about a guy that ugly is at least he's not a scammer who stole a male model's photo."

Hailey squinted to get a better look at the profile photo. "He's not that ugly."

Julie glanced up at her. "Would you go out with him?"

"Oh, look," she said, "Somebody's sent you a message. Two in fact. Click through."

Julia did. *"Bigbrownbear?* His handle is Bigbrownbear? I am so going into a nunnery." She clicked the message open anyway. It showed a man who could have been one of Santa's elves. His profile stated he was sixty, but he appeared a decade older. "Not big, not brown, not a bear. My luck continues," Julia said.

"He's a sculptor," Hailey read. "That's interesting. He says he'd like to meet for coffee."

"Maybe he wants to adopt me."

"Oh, look, another message just came through."

"From hotboy." She clicked the email icon and up came the message. She read aloud. "Lookin for a rockin' older gal. Do you go for younger guys?"

No one said a word when she clicked Delete.

"Okay, let's try John2012."

"What do you bet his name isn't even John?" Julia clicked on the message. A nice face looked out at them from the guy's profile photo. He'd sent a short message that said he'd be interested in getting to know her a little better.

Instead of deleting him, Julia clicked through to the man's online profile. He said he was recently divorced and worked in the computer industry. His hobbies included sailing, ethnic restaurants and reading. Hailey held her tongue and waited for Julia's verdict.

"He looks boring," she said. "And he has no style."

Hailey read over her friend's shoulder. "He sounds nice. And you both like to eat out. You have that in common. What have you got to lose?"

"He probably thinks Frank Gehry is a football player."

"Julia, at least meet the guy for coffee."

"Hmm. I don't know." All the same she pulled up each of his three photos and studied them.

"Julia, go for coffee with this man. It's only coffee."

"What if we hate each other on sight?"

"Order an espresso so you can gulp it down if you have to. You can always talk about books."

"I don't know." Julia made to close her laptop. Hailey prevented her. "Do it. Send him a message back. Immediately."

"You are so bossy. If I have a terrible time I'm billing you at my hourly rate."

She squeezed her friend's shoulder. "There's someone wonderful out there for you. I know it."

Rob said, "Let me take a look."

Both women stared at him. "You're interested in Julia's matches? Maybe you and Bigbrownbear have a future."

"Very funny. I want to look at Julia's profile."

"Why?"

"What is it with you two? I'm a guy. In the right age range. I can tell you if your profile's any good."

"I don't want to appeal to you. No offense, but I wouldn't date you."

"None taken. I wouldn't date you either." He held out his hand. "Now give."

Hailey brought Julia's profile back up and handed over the tablet. He took his time, read everything she'd written and perused the three photos. Then he shook his head. "You come across as boring, too. This isn't you."

Julia tapped her fingernails on the tabletop. "Like I said, you're not my target market."

"What's bothering you about her profile?" Hailey asked. Maybe he and Julia wouldn't ever date each other but he was right. He was a man in the same age range. Also he was smart and well-traveled.

"The photograph is too businesslike. I bet it's the one you use on your staging website, isn't it?"

"Absolutely. I paid a lot of money for a professional portrait. Why not use it?"

"Because you're not selling your services as a stager, you're selling yourself as a sexual partner and possible marriage material. The business suit and heavy makeup aren't cutting it."

"But—"

"Wait right there." He got to his feet, grabbed his cane and limped over to his camera bag, taking out a smallish SLR camera and came back toward her.

"What are you doing?" Julia sounded alarmed and looked to Hailey for help.

"I'm taking your picture."

She flapped her hands. "I'm not dressed right. My makeup's terrible."

"You look great. You look like yourself."

Hailey nodded. "I agree. You dress with such great Bohemian style. You've got your favorite dangly earrings on, you're wearing a colorful sweater and you are having a good hair day. Swipe on some more lip gloss and you'll look fab."

After they'd both convinced Julia she didn't have

to post Rob's pictures if she didn't like them, they persuaded her to go into the living room and stand by the arrangement of flowers as colorful and vibrant as she was.

He got Hailey to move a lamp and then went to work snapping photos. He gave her quiet instructions about moving her chin down and what to do with her hands. He had her turn her body a little and Hailey watched her friend relax and get into the mood of the photo shoot. "Think about the greatest sex you've ever had," he said as he focused.

Julia's face softened and her smile grew intimate. *Wow,* Hailey thought, watching him bend and move, totally focused on his task. He might be injured, but everything apart from his leg was athletic, virile. She could imagine having the greatest sex ever with Rob. In fact it was all she could think about.

Damn. She had a problem.

He snapped a few more photos and then nodded.

"Okay. I'll email you the best of these and you can post a new profile picture. I guarantee it will help. Also, maybe make your written profile more—I don't know—personal. A guy's not too interested in where you went to school."

"What does he want to know?" Hailey asked.

"Will she be fun to be with? How much baggage is she dragging around? Does she play games? Is she looking for her kids' daddy? Is she sane? You know, stuff like that."

"Great," Julia said, pretending to type. "I'm fun to be with, the only games I play are Scrabble and Monopoly, I may want kids someday but there's no hurry, I'm a little bit crazy, but in a good way."

"Yep, that works. Only, substitute strip poker for Monopoly if you really want to pull."

She giggled. "Thanks. I'll get you one of my business cards so you can email me the photos."

He turned, still grinning, toward Hailey. "How about you? You want me to take some shots of you?"

"For what? A dating site?"

He shrugged, his eyes both teasing and challenging. "Sure, why not?"

She couldn't hold his gaze. Instead she began fussing with the flower arrangement. "I don't have time to date. I have a career to build."

She heard the snapping of the camera and glared at him. "What are you doing?"

"Candid photos. You might want something for your website. You look good with those flowers."

"Oh. Okay."

Julia returned, handed over one of her business cards and Rob slipped it into his wallet. "I guarantee plenty more Bigbrownbears will be beating down your door when you fix your profile."

"I can hardly wait."

Then she turned to Hailey. "Come on. We'd better get to work upstairs."

Hailey nodded. "And you, Rob, can make yourself scarce."

"Thrown out of my own home," he muttered, then looked at Hailey. "And I'm a cripple. What kind of woman throws a cripple out?"

"A woman who wants to sell this house."

He repacked his camera bag and then grabbed his cane. He'd been using the cane, she noted, on a regular basis and neither of them had mentioned it. She was glad he had it in him to be a little bit sensible.

They'd been working together only a few days but she'd started to look forward to coming here. She liked Bellamy House, liked its history, the neighborhood, its possibilities.

And, in spite of his annoying quirks, she liked the house's current owner.

When he looked at her with those white teeth set in his tanned face she thought maybe she liked the current owner a little too much.

"Have a nice afternoon," she called when he stomped out, making his limp as pronounced as possible.

"Don't sell my house to any losers."

7

JULIA'S HOPES WERE so low when she entered Beananza for her first actual date with a real man from LoveMatch.com that if they'd been any lower she'd still be in bed.

What was she even doing here? All right for Hailey to talk her into emailing the only man who seemed remotely in her dating range since she wasn't the one feeling like a complete fool.

The only thing that made a quick coffee with a complete stranger acceptable was that she could drink her favorite brew in her favorite location.

When the door banged behind her, she breathed in the coffee smell and glanced around.

She saw him right away, John2012. Sitting by himself at a table for two, a china mug in front of him. She glanced at the old-fashioned clock on the wall and realized she was ten minutes late. Oops.

She headed toward him and he stood up and held out his hand. "Hi. I'm John." Nice firm grip. At least she'd give him that.

"I'm Julia."

"I thought you'd stood me up," he said.

"No. Sorry, I guess I'm running a couple of minutes late." She glanced down at his half-finished coffee. "Were you early?"

"I like to be on time," he said.

"Oh." *This is going well.* She took a step toward the coffee bar, Hailey's suggestion of a quick espresso in her mind when he said, "What can I get you?"

"Oh, thanks. Tall, skinny latte."

"Coming right up."

He walked to the bar and she had a chance to study him. He was on the slim side but tall with muscular shoulders. There was something almost cowboy about him with his weathered skin, two deep lines running down lean cheeks, deep blue eyes and a prominent nose and chin. But who dressed him? That blue plaid shirt, faded from washing, was older than some of her friends. The jeans were the most unflattering she'd ever seen and had to be from a discount store, and when he'd stepped into a pair of truly ugly work shoe/boot things, he'd caught the back hems of the denim in them.

If he'd paid more than six dollars for that haircut he'd been ripped off since she suspected the barber learned his trade in an abattoir.

When John put in her drink order, Bruno glanced over and waved.

John sauntered back to her reminding her again oddly of a cowboy. All he needed was a Stetson and a way nicer pair of jeans. He set the mugs carefully on the table and she thanked him politely. Then almost choked.

Bruno's latte art topping her brew today was a question mark.

She gulped her coffee quickly, hoping John hadn't noticed. If she ever did this again she'd meet in an anonymous coffee chain store. One that served to-go cups in case she needed to make a quick exit.

They both sipped coffee and then he said, "This is a nice place. I haven't been here before."

"I like it. The coffee's good."

Silence. Oh, man, this was tougher than she'd imagined. She loved new people. Always prided herself on being able to talk to anyone, and here she was acting like a self-conscious fool. She had to get a grip.

So many of her friends and family were getting married, having kids, moving on with their lives. Was she becoming desperate? She hated the thought.

She tried to recall John's profile so she could at least start some kind of conversation. "So, you like ethnic restaurants?"

"I do," he nodded. "One thing we have in common."

"Do you have favorites?"

He shook his head, looking grim. "My ex only liked fancy high-end places. I didn't get much chance to try out smaller, ethnic places." Then he winced. "Sorry. Great start to a first date. Talk about your angry, bitter divorce."

"Was it?"

"Angry and bitter?" he shrugged. "Is there another kind?"

"I don't know. I've never been married."

They both took refuge in another sip of coffee.

"How 'bout you? I bet you eat out a lot?"

What? Was he suggesting she was so overweight she must spend all her free time grazing at all-you-can-eat buffets?

"No," she said. "Not really."

"Oh. You seem really cosmopolitan, as though you

know all the good places." He seemed a little disappointed to find out she wasn't that person.

But she *was* that person. She supposed she'd become so freaked out by the scammer that she wasn't giving a perfectly nice man a chance.

She glanced up and caught his gaze, realizing he was as uncomfortable as she. All of a sudden Bruno's caffeinated question mark, the pressure of too many friends' marriages and babies, the scammer, all of it seemed so ridiculous, she started to laugh. "I don't know about you but I'd really like to start over."

He nodded. "Can we consider that bitter-divorce comment deleted?"

"Done."

He let out a sigh of relief, and leaned back in his chair. And it was better. For no reason except that they'd been honest for a moment, it was better.

"Your profile said you work in computers?"

"That's right. I'm a programmer. My team works on software for the construction industry."

"Oh. I'm a home stager. That's sort of related to the construction industry."

"The way high fashion is connected to the silkworm."

"Okay. You made me smile. That's good."

So they talked about their respective businesses and she realized her coffee mug was empty and she hadn't had a terrible time.

"Well?" he asked, and she was reminded of Bruno's question mark.

"Well?" she asked back.

"You seem like a nice woman. I'd like to see you again if you're interested. Maybe we could try out one of those ethnic restaurants we both like."

Her silence dragged on a second too long while she processed the bad hair, bad clothes, and tried to imagine herself showing up to a decent restaurant with him at her side.

"I'm not sure we'd be a fit," she finally said, as honestly as she could without hurting his feelings, she hoped.

He didn't seem crushed. He merely nodded. "Tell you what, I'm not a big fan of emailing through a dating site. Here's my card with my personal email and my cell phone. If you ever want a friend to have dinner with or somebody to take in a movie or something, go ahead and call me."

She took the card and tucked it into her bag. "Thanks."

He rose and shook her hand again. "You heading out?" he motioned to the door.

She couldn't stand the idea of making small talk as they headed outside to their vehicles so she shook her head. "I'll have another coffee and check my email."

He nodded. "I enjoyed meeting you. Good luck." And was gone.

Since Bruno currently had nothing more pressing to do than fill the canisters with sugar, she walked up to him and said, "Well? What did you think?"

When Bruno turned to her he was wearing a T-shirt sporting a cup of coffee with these words printed on the surface: *Black as the devil, hot as hell, pure as an angel, sweet as love. Talleyrand.*

"Seemed like a nice guy. He a new squeeze?"

"No. I don't think so. We met online. This was the first time we'd seen each other in person."

"He's tall."

"Dresses badly."

"Mmm."

"He told me to call him if I want to go to dinner or a movie. I didn't feel much chemistry, but he seems like an okay guy. What do you think? Should I call him?"

Bruno neatened the packages on top of a silver canister. "Depends how desperate you get, I guess."

THE STATUE OF LENIN had been standing in the middle of Fremont for almost twenty years now, Rob supposed, as he wandered killing time, while strangers toured his grandmother's house.

He scowled at Lenin.

Lenin scowled back.

Rob still remembered the fuss when a local businessman bought the huge bronze statue and transported it to Seattle with the help of the original sculptor. Designed and installed in Czechoslovakia, the piece had fallen victim to the Velvet Revolution and would have been sold for scrap had not an English teacher from Washington agreed to buy it, perceiving it not as propaganda but as a work of art. He wondered how poor old Vladimir would feel if he could see the way Fremont treated his likeness.

He'd been decorated with Christmas lights, dressed up to resemble John Lennon and even dressed in drag for Gay Pride week. Today he was standing fairly peacefully, his revolutionary torch before him, Western capitalism surrounding him in the form of stores and restaurants, and trees blushing red as autumn deepened.

Rob had his camera bag slung over his shoulder, more out of habit than because he'd had any real intention of snapping photos. He'd learned long ago that a working photographer is always on. If a giant meteor fell out of the sky and crushed Lenin, he'd kill himself if he'd been right here, an eyewitness, and had missed documenting the event.

Not that any meteors seemed to be in sight. The sky was clear and sunny, unusual for fall in Seattle. The mild weather had brought people out to walk and chat and stroll.

Apart from tourists, nobody paid much attention to the formidable statue, all going about their business, living their lives. Once again he experienced that odd feeling of the similarity of most people's lives and concerns no matter where they live. Here came a mother chastising her son for something. The kid's expression was so bored as he slouched along at her side, Rob had his camera out before he realized his intention.

He forgot the pain in his leg, forgot his enforced exile from work, forgot the annoyance of two bossy women trying to sell his grandmother's house with the maximum disturbance to him, forgot even the inconvenience of his strong attraction to his uppity Realtor.

He snapped photos, tiny frozen moments in time, knowing the best ones would tell a story, evoke an emotion, bring strangers together in one fleeting moment of recognition. Maybe it was good for him to have this time. He discovered that without the heat of conflict, which was usually the environment in which he worked, he had more time to frame and set up shots, wait for the perfect moment.

The wobble of the chocolate gelato balanced precariously on a toddler's cone while mom and an older woman, maybe grandma, chatted together, the lick that sent the scoop tumbling, the splat, the wail of grief and despair.

The fussing women, the kid's tears.

He'd seen enough of kids' tears that he couldn't do

anything about but report whatever conflict the inno-
cents had been caught in. This he could fix.

He quickly walked into the ice-cream store, paid for
a replacement cone and made the teenage boy working
behind the counter in a striped apron deliver it so there'd
be no misunderstandings. No embarrassing gratitude.

He got his reward when the little kid stopped crying
and took the brand-new cone with a hiccup and a lisped
thanks, his heartbreak melting faster than the lump of
ice cream on the pavement.

When Rob next checked the time, the sun was setting
and he saw on his watch that two hours had passed with
the speed of minutes. He packed up his bag, gripped
his grandmother's cane and made his slow way to his
grandmother's old Buick which he'd jump-started since
the battery had gone dead.

He had no idea what he was going to do with the images he'd captured today, but he had the pleasant sensation of a good day's work.

He decided to reward himself with a good meal of
the freshest Pacific Northwest ingredients. If he bought
enough food for two, that was his business.

And since he was in town only for a short time, he
carefully drove his grandmother's Buick to Pike Place
Market. The place was bustling as usual and smelled of
spices mixed with coffee mixed with the scents of arti-
sanal cheeses and fresh flowers, all flowing around him
and interweaving with memories of souks and farmer's
markets all over the world.

His camera trigger finger began to itch until he gave
in and once more pulled out his equipment. The personality of Pike's was as individual as the souks of Mar-
rakech and yet...

He spent a happy thirty minutes or so loading up

on fresh ingredients for dinner. Because he was an optimist, he even bought wine. Which he would never drink alone.

WHEN HE ARRIVED HOME, Rob was pleased to see the lights were still on in the house. That meant Hailey was probably waiting for him.

Sure enough when he opened the front door and limped inside she came out of the kitchen with her suit jacket on and her bag in her hand.

"I was waiting for you," she said.

"So I see." He lifted the sack of groceries. "I'm cooking if you want to stay for dinner."

She fiddled with the button on her jacket. Glanced up at him, blushed and glanced back down. He was cold, tired and his leg throbbed but one glance from those blue-gray eyes and he was transported back to their steamy session in the bedroom.

"I—um— Maybe we should talk," she said.

"Uh-huh?" He put down his bags, slipped off his jacket and hung it on the old oak coat tree she'd stripped bare before the customers arrived, though if you asked him, a coat tree with no coats on it looked a damned sight stranger than one with a coat or two hanging from it.

"Dinner is, uh, unexpected."

"Not when it's dinnertime."

She gripped the handle of her briefcase. "What happened…" She stumbled to a halt and for some reason, he began to enjoy himself.

"You mean the kissing?"

He leaned against the wall, partly so he could take the weight off his injured leg and partly so he could watch her face.

"Yes. Yes. The kissing." She looked adorable, sexy, unsure, confused, a little irritated. "It was very unprofessional." She fiddled with that button some more. "It won't happen again."

Good. That was excellent news. Whatever crazy bug had bitten the pair of them, they'd both obviously come to their senses. Getting involved with a high-strung Realtor who was attempting to sell his house was a terrible idea. He'd had some bad ones, and this was up there with the worst.

So why did he have to be perverse? Why couldn't he simply agree it was a bad idea, shake her hand and promise to keep his distance if she kept hers?

Because he was a born fool, that's why. And kissing her again might be a bad idea, but not kissing her again seemed infinitely worse. "It won't happen again?"

She shook her head. "No."

"But what if I want it to happen again?"

Her lips quirked at that, and he could see her trying to reel in the smile. "I'm your Realtor. Our relationship has to be strictly professional."

"I see."

He regarded her for a moment, crossed his arms in front of his chest. "I suppose I could fire you."

8

"FIRE ME?" Hailey could not believe the words she'd just heard. It was the last thing she'd expected to come out of his mouth. In fact, she'd expected that he'd be as eager as she to put that unfortunate incident behind them.

At least she knew she would if she could only stop thinking about it.

It wasn't fair. She had plans. Two agendas keeping her life and her future on track. And nowhere, not in the electronic minder and not in the paper backup did she have time slotted in for a personal relationship.

Okay, she knew that these things happened in their own time. Of course she did. But her attraction to Rob wasn't only inconvenient in its timing, it was horrible on every level. Even if she could stand the idea of a relationship with a man when she really didn't have time for it, she would never choose a guy like Rob. Never. Not in a million years. He was everything she didn't want in a man. Restless. A wanderer. She'd had enough of wandering men.

With a father who'd moved his family twelve years out of thirteen she understood her need for stability. The very notion of being with a man who had those same itchy feet was inconceivable.

Her ideal man was a stay-put kind of guy—the kind whose idea of fun was puttering in the garden, working on home-building projects. A thrilling Saturday date would be wandering around a home-improvement store hand in hand, good-naturedly arguing about Brazilian cherrywood for the foyer as opposed to reclaiming the original oak. Naturally, they'd end up reclaiming the oak. She loved old houses that kept their original features. In her mind, Brazilian cherrywood should grace the homes of Brazilians.

Rob's idea of a Saturday afternoon was shooting footage of rebels in a country most people couldn't find on a map, never mind pronounce, and then getting shot himself.

So, in spite of the fact that one steamy kiss had disordered her plans, and intruded on her daydreams—and, okay, her night dreams, too, she had to be clear that it couldn't happen again. Once she'd told him that there'd be no future physical contact between the two of them, she was certain she'd stop thinking about it herself.

All he had to do was agree with her, maybe even apologize for getting carried away, though she knew perfectly well she'd been as crazed as he had. She blushed even to recall her own actions.

And did he make it easy for her?

Did he agree there'd be no future contact?

Did he apologize?

Hell no. He threatened to fire her. And with the most foolish, sexy grin on his face while he did it.

"You can't fire me."

"I believe I can."

"But—" Even though she knew he was toying with

her she still felt irritation pound through her veins. Why couldn't he make this easy for her? "But—" She shook her head. "You're not going to fire me."

He seemed to consider her words carefully. "No. But I probably want to kiss you again. Assuming you want to kiss me again, too, I don't think we should let a dumb thing like business get in the way."

"I don't want to kiss you again," she blurted, feeling more ridiculous by the second as this absurd conversation continued.

"Then we don't have a problem."

"Good. Okay."

He didn't argue, didn't fight for the opportunity to kiss her so senseless she could barely see straight. That was good. That was excellent.

"I still think you should have dinner with me."

She was so busy thinking of all the scorching kissing they weren't going to be doing that his request threw her. "What?"

He grinned at her. Leaning against the wall looking sexier than any man should.

"Have dinner with me."

"When?"

"Tonight."

"You're asking me for a date? Didn't you hear a single word I just said?"

"I'm not asking you for a date. I stopped at Pike Place Market and bought fresh sockeye, asparagus and potatoes. Seems like too nice a meal to eat alone."

She narrowed her eyes at him. "You don't know how to cook, do you? You want me to make you dinner."

"I happen to be an excellent cook."

"I'm not—"

"And you can tell me all about your showing today."

For some reason he was much cheerier than when he'd left hours earlier, and the feeling was oddly contagious.

"How come you came back in such a good mood? You were a complete grump when you left."

"When you kicked me out of my own home, you mean." He reached down and grabbed the white plastic grocery sack off the floor and started on his halting way to the kitchen. "I had an epiphany this afternoon."

"An epiphany? Don't tell me. You realized how lucky you are to have Seattle's finest Realtor at your beck and call?"

He turned to glance at her over his shoulder. "I thought becking and calling were out, as per our professional relationship."

She had to bite back an answering smile. He was just so easy to be with, so easy to flirt with, damn it. "So you *were* listening."

"Oh, I heard you all right. I just don't happen to agree with you. I think you can mix business and pleasure and make both more interesting. But that's me."

"Have you ever—" she began and then could have bitten her tongue. What was she thinking?

Having reached the kitchen he put down the sack and turned on the kitchen faucet to wash his hands. "Have I ever had a relationship with a work colleague? Sure. Haven't you?"

The stab of—what? Surely not jealousy—surprised her. It wasn't any of her business who he got involved with.

"No. Never."

He turned off the tap and dried his hands. Nice hands, she noted. Long-fingered and strong.

"How about a client? Have you ever been involved with a client?"

"Romantically?"

Even though his face was serious, his eyes laughed at her. "Yeah, romantically."

Apart from him? "No. I told you. I set rules for myself."

"Didn't you ever hear that nice old saying about rules being meant to be broken?"

"I bet you've broken a few rules in your time."

He chuckled. "One or two." He reached for the bottom of a set of three drawers and drew out an apron with the ease of somebody who's done it frequently. It was green cotton with sprigs of yellow flowers; obviously one of his grandmother's. When he popped the bib over his head and tied the string around his waist without any worry about whether he looked ridiculous or not, her heart melted a little.

He didn't look a bit ridiculous. He looked comfortable in his skin and his grandmother's apron which made her think he was also comfortable with his memories of her. Nice.

She removed her suit jacket, hung it over the back of one of the kitchen chairs, and then rolled up the sleeves of her silk blouse. "What can I do?"

He was taking items out of the bag. He placed a bottle of wine on the counter. "Can you open the wine?"

"Sure."

He'd bought wine. She wondered if this impromptu dinner date was actually planned. And whether she minded.

She opened the wine—a Washington pinot noir—and poured it into two glasses she found in the cupboard he gestured to.

"What else?"

"Want to sous-chef?"

"Why not?"

He reached for the drawer and took out a second apron. This one was cream sprigged with pink roses. He shook it out and then held the top strap for her, waiting until she stepped closer before looping it over her head. He turned her around, putting his hands on her hips in a gesture that was probably cheflike, but felt ridiculously intimate.

She was deeply aware of his hands moving behind her as he straightened the straps. "My grandmother was a little more stout than you," he said, and then brought his arms around her middle, doubling the straps around her waist. She felt him so close to her, felt his breath on her neck as he fastened the ties at her back. She wanted badly to lean against him, let the attraction she felt for him take them wherever it led.

"All done," he said, stepping away and breaking the spell.

"Thanks."

He passed her the asparagus and potatoes and, as she snapped the ends off the former and scrubbed the latter, he prepared a sauce for the salmon.

They worked companionably, side by side in the kitchen. "I bought a decent barbecue last time I was here. It's about the only modern thing in the place. I'll grill the salmon."

"Where did you learn to cook?" she asked.

"From my grandmother. Long before it became trendy she thought every man should be able to cook. The first time she saw Jamie Oliver on TV she said to me, 'There you are, Rob. I told you so. Men who cook make women swoon.'"

Hailey laughed. "Did she really say *swoon?*"

"Absolutely. I swear she actually did swoon when he started that program to get healthier lunches in schools. She was a former English teacher, you know."

"I didn't."

"You'd have liked her. I think she'd have liked you, too."

"I'm glad."

He reminded her a bit of one of those sexy celebrity chefs. Casual, assured, not bothering to measure things very precisely, but fully in control. She'd never seen a man in a flowered apron look so handsome.

"Do you cook much?" she asked.

"I don't cook when I'm away, and when I'm in New York I mostly eat out. With so many good restaurants, you could eat out every night and never get bored. I do most of my cooking here. In this kitchen."

He glanced around. "I'm glad you stayed. It's weird being here without her, you know?"

"I can imagine."

To lighten the atmosphere she said, "I'll set the table."

He looked at her as though she were crazy. "It's already set."

"The table's staged. You can't eat off this stuff or mess up the placemats and napkins. Julia would kill us both."

"My grandmother would not approve of staging," he said.

"If your grandmother was as smart as you make her out to be she'd love anything that got her more money for her house."

She knew she had him when he shook his head. "Damn, she really would have liked you."

"You miss her, don't you?" Stupid question, but sometimes she found the dumbest question was the right one.

His mouth twisted. "I keep thinking I'll hear her voice. She used to phone me sometimes but the biggest thrill was when she emailed me the first time." He chuckled at the memory. "She must have been eighty-two. She bought a computer and hired a kid to teach her how to use it. She wanted to surprise me. And hell, did she ever. I was checking my email in Istanbul and there's a message from her."

"Wow."

"I know. Funny thing is she always wrote emails as though they were formal letters. You know, 'Dearest Robert, I hope this finds you well.' That kind of thing. I got such a kick out of them." It would be a long time before he stopped expecting her to call him or, to his intense delight, email him. He caught himself before he went on. "Anyhow, she was a cool lady. And she had no time for men who were useless around the house. Therefore, I cook."

As she'd suspected, dinner was perfectly cooked. Simple and delicious.

The placemats were faded with age and the dishes clearly had been frequently used, in contrast to the designer linens and gleaming Denby china Julia had provided.

Once he'd lit a couple of candles, the atmosphere was cozy, romantic even, though she pushed the word out of her mind the second she thought it.

When she bit into the salmon she almost moaned with pleasure. "This is fantastic."

"So? Was my grandmother right? Am I the next Jamie Oliver?"

"Jamie Oliver doesn't wear flowered aprons."

He shrugged. "He has his style. I have mine."

Privately, she liked Rob's style. Which was a problem.

She did not want to have romantic feelings for Rob.

Which immediately reminded that she was not here for pleasure, in spite of the mouthwatering meal and good wine, but for business.

"I think the people who came today really liked the house."

He speared a potato. "Did they?"

"Yes. A nice family relocating from Connecticut."

"Hmm."

"You have a problem with Easterners?"

He chewed his potato. Swallowed. "No. Not at all."

"Good. The company transferring them is putting them up for three days in a hotel and in that time they hope to make a decision. They'd want a fairly quick closing date so they can move their family in and he can start his new job."

"How quick are we talking?"

"It's negotiable, of course, but I think a quick closing would be a big selling feature. They want their kids settled in before the school year is too advanced."

"Hmm. What happened to that other couple? The ones who interrupted my sleep?"

"The MacDonalds?"

"Yeah."

"They didn't like the angry presence in the house."

He laid down his knife and fork and drilled her with his gaze. "My grandmother would never haunt anyone. And she was never negative."

She sent him a thin smile. "They were talking about you."

"Weenies. The house wasn't right for them."

In fact she knew it was but what was the point of arguing? She hoped the Fergusons, Ted and Sue, and their three kids aged eight to thirteen might soon call Bellamy House home. Not only was she anxious to close a sale, but she was beginning to think that the less time she spent with Rob the better.

"I expect to hear from them tomorrow. They may want to view the property a second time. I hope you can accommodate them."

"Kicking me out again?"

"Believe me, as soon as the deal closes, you will be left in peace."

"Are you kidding me? I have to figure out what to do with all this stuff." He gestured vaguely around the kitchen, which she knew meant the things in drawers and cupboards that the stagers hadn't removed. Not to mention all the furniture and items currently in storage.

"You know, there are charities that could make good use of her things. And the valuable or sentimental pieces you could put into storage until you decide what you want to keep. I could put you in touch with the right people."

He nodded.

"Well," she said, "I hate to eat and run but I've got some paperwork I'd like to do tonight. I'll let you know when I hear back from the Fergusons' Realtor."

"You do that."

He got to his feet and, using the cane, followed her to the front door.

She turned to bid him goodbye and found him closer

than she'd have dreamed possible. He could really move with that cane.

"Thank you again—"

"About that kissing thing," he interrupted. Were they back to that again?

"What about the kissing thing?" she asked, half irritated, half intrigued.

"I want to give you some more information."

"More information? About kissing?"

"Not exactly. More about other things." He dropped his gaze to the cane. "I want you to know, in case you're wondering, that the bullet damaged some muscle and nicked a bone. Nothing that won't heal. Everything else is in perfect working order." He raised his gaze to hers. "In case you were wondering."

"I wasn't." Mostly because it had been perfectly obvious from their kissing that everything was working fine. As he must know.

"And about that kissing thing—"

"Oh, for heaven's sake. Would you forget about the kissing thing?"

She felt his nearness, his warmth, the stirrings of desire.

"No. Some things are unforgettable."

A tiny sound came out of her throat, unbidden, primal. Their gazes connected and it was like a match to dry tinder.

Her heart sped up, her skin began to tingle.

He moved closer; their mouths were in easy reach. With no order from any thinking part of her brain, her lips parted.

He moved closer. "I want to tell you that since you're

the one with the rules I'm going to leave the next move
to you."

While she stood there astonished, he leaned past her
to open the door. "Good night."

9

ROB WAS BEGINNING to find his forced sabbatical much more interesting than he'd ever anticipated, he thought, as he lugged his camera bag awkwardly down the old wooden steps to the unfinished basement. The smell of the lower floor was as familiar to him as a signature perfume on a woman. It smelled like dust and aging cement and years of layered memory. Down here he'd built his first model airplane with newspaper spread out to catch the glue drips though somehow they always ended up on him anyway. He supposed he'd had a man cave back before the term even existed. A boy cave in truth. A lumpy old couch still crouched in the corner. He'd hunched on it on rainy Saturday afternoons to read comic books. Later he'd snuck a girl or two down here for some heavy petting. And in between all of that his grandmother had allowed him to turn an old bathroom into a darkroom.

Now that his home had become a decorator's showplace everywhere but down here, he'd begun using the old oak desk in the corner. He fired up his computer and downloaded today's photos.

He began looking through his personal photo library,

hunting for the similarities he'd detected between these everyday scenes in the town he called home and the many scenes of daily life he'd witnessed in places far, far from home.

He'd read somewhere that the different racial characteristics had developed around ten thousand years ago. Before that man had been one small tribe in Africa. He'd begun to realize what human DNA demonstrated—we are more similar than we are different.

Over the next couple of weeks he worked on his idea. It gave shape to his days, a purpose to his idleness. He'd never in all his career had time like this to devote to a larger project. He'd become so accustomed to snatching a story in process, snapping photos that were more about capturing today's action than art. Now he had the time and leisure to do both. And to tell a story that wouldn't be old news in a few weeks but was timeless.

He'd caught up with a few of his old friends, and it was strange to see them settled, some with families.

"Still footloose and fancy-free, huh?" Mike Lazenby asked him as they hung out at Mike's place one Saturday afternoon while his wife shopped. The guy was pacing the living room, a squirming, fussy infant draped over his shoulder. A line of spit-up ran down his back like seagull poop. But there was no jealousy in his tone. While Mike had been a legendary womanizer and rabble-rouser back in the day, Rob sensed deep contentment in his old friend.

"Yep."

Wouldn't be his choice, but it was nice to see Mike happy.

He saw Hailey a few times whenever she dropped in to make sure the place was perfect before she booted him out for her showings. He took perverse pride in always being there, in making her boot him out. It was kind of a kick, as was the buzz of electricity between them every time they saw each other.

He was healing nicely. He was well rested, well fed and in far too frequent company with the sexiest Realtor he'd ever seen. He wondered when they were going to close the deal between each other.

From how she looked at him from time to time, he knew, whether she said so or not, that she was thinking the same thing.

She'd been pretty pissed with him when he'd told the Fergusons—truthfully—that raccoons nested in the trees in his yard. He used to have one that climbed right up to his window where he'd leave food out for it. Okay, maybe he'd overheard the little girl say she was scared of raccoons but he was certain that wasn't the only reason they'd chosen another home. He wasn't disappointed to lose out on a fast sale that would have left him homeless as well as jobless.

Since she'd found them another home and closed the deal, she'd gotten over that. Still, he had to be careful or firing her wouldn't be an issue. She'd quit.

It was a rainy Thursday and once again he was pushed out of his own home.

"Where are you going in this rain with a camera?" she asked him.

"I have a date with a troll," he told her.

She raised her brows but she had to know he meant Fremont's very own troll, the sculpture under the Aurora Bridge, which he was going to photograph. He had no idea what he was going to do, but was confident that creativity, luck and timing would be on his side.

Or else he'd go get a coffee at Beananza and read the paper.

"Have fun with your troll."

"I'd rather have fun with you. You thought anymore about that kissing thing?"

The door shut with a decided bang behind him. He chuckled. Trolls could turn up anywhere.

He got lucky. Some tourists had come to see the troll and after he took a few snaps of them with their camera, he asked if he could take a few with his. One day they might be published, he told them, though it would probably be on his website. If he ever got one started.

Then the Adopt-a-Troll group came by to clean up litter. He snapped a few more shots. And finally he photographed the gloomy guy all alone beneath the cavernous bridge.

He still had time to stop for a coffee before heading home.

HAILEY HADN'T BOTHERED to tell Rob that the family coming to view the place today were cousins of Julia's. It wasn't any of his business. Paige and Jay were expecting their first child. Likely the house was out of their price range but even if it was they might tell friends about the place. Hal Wilson at work was about to list a very nice town house that would suit Paige and Jay and a little one perfectly.

Naturally, when the doorbell rang there were more than two people standing there. Paige and Jay, Julia, Paige's sister Noreen and Julia's mother Gloria were already talking a mile a minute as she opened the door.

"Congratulations on the listing, honey," Gloria said, giving her a huge hug. Gloria was an older, heavier version of Julia. Dramatic, outspoken and deeply maternal.

"Thanks. Julia's staging really makes the house shine."

"I couldn't be more proud of you two." Hailey knew it was true and once more felt very fortunate to be considered part of this loving family.

"Come on in and see the house," she said.

The oohs and aahs were predictable. As was the moment when Paige said, "I feel overwhelmed. This place is too big."

Hailey nodded. "I think I have the ideal place for you. It's not even on the market yet. We can see it tomorrow."

She described the town house and immediately saw the couple exchange glances and nod. "Let's see it," Jay said. "I'd be a lot happier with a mortgage I could pay off in this lifetime."

"Since you're here, you've got to see upstairs. The master bedroom is my dream room."

While Julia showed Paige and Jay the rest of the upstairs, Gloria remained with Hailey in the big master bedroom, admiring the view of the backyard, the fireplace and the window seat. "What a beautiful room." She walked to the four-poster. "And the bed!"

"I know." Every time she was in this room Hailey experienced a sense of connection she couldn't understand. She'd simply come to accept it. She'd step into the room and immediately feel that it was somehow hers, her fantasies of her and Rob in that bed as vivid as though they were memories.

"Agnes Neeson was my English teacher in high school," Gloria remarked.

"Really? Was she a good teacher?"

"The best." She shook her head. "Her daughter was a real mess though. She dropped out of high school. Always in trouble. Sex, drugs and rock and roll. Poor Mrs. Neeson. It was really sad."

"That would be Rob's mother."

"The current owner?"

She nodded.

"How did he turn out?"

"He's… He's…" How to describe Rob? "He's a successful photojournalist. Works for *World Week*." Without thinking, she sat on the bed and Gloria joined her. "He's driven, ambitious, cares about people."

"Easy on the eyes."

"Oh, yeah."

"You two having sex yet?"

"Gloria!"

"What? You think I don't know you almost as well as my own kids? You're crazy about the man. I can hear it in your voice."

"I've thought about it." She blew out a breath. "I can barely think about anything else. But there'd be no future."

"I've never known a woman who spent so much time worrying about the future as you do. Maybe you should try living for now a little more." The older woman drilled her with a gaze that was like Julia's only with more life experience. "Have you had sex even once since your engagement broke up?"

She shook her head.

"Maybe it's time."

A shiver ran through her. Maybe it was.

"What if I fall in love with him and he breaks my heart?"

"You're doing it again. Forget the future and start living for today." She nudged Hailey with her elbow. "Or tonight."

Hailey knew herself too well to believe she could have an affair and not end up hurt. Maybe Gloria was right though. What if she indulged herself and Rob? Not for a long time, that could be dangerous.

But for a short time? Just to give in to the attraction that burned between them?

Could she play with fire and not get burned?

Maybe just one night.

THE LIGHTS WERE ON, as Rob had expected they'd be when he returned home from Beananza. Hailey always waited to tell him how her showing had gone. He liked to think she enjoyed their short visits as much as he did.

Remembering the door slam as he'd left, he called out, "Hi, honey. I'm home."

She came from the direction of the kitchen looking better than any Realtor should. He really wished she'd quit making them both wait for something she must know was inevitable.

Something seemed different about her. She glowed with suppressed excitement. With a sense of foreboding he prayed she wasn't going to present an offer on the house.

"How was the showing?"

"It wasn't right for them. Young couple with a child on the way. They need something smaller."

"Too bad," he said even as a feeling of relief slid through him.

If she hadn't sold his house, what was she looking so excited about?

"How's your leg?"

"Healing. Why?" He glanced at her with suspicion. "If you have some big-ass box that needs moving or furniture to unload I have to remind you I'm the walking wounded."

"What if I want sex?"

He was so dumbfounded he put all his weight on his bad leg and nearly went down. "What did you say?"

"It's a purely theoretical question. I was wondering whether you think your leg is strong enough for you to have sex?"

"Yes." The answer was definite.

"Theoretically yes?"

"Let's-go-upstairs-and-rip-our-clothes-off yes."

Hailey was enjoying herself. It wasn't a big surprise he'd so enthusiastically said yes. In fact, she'd have been stunned if he hadn't, given the level of sizzle between them recently. But to have amazed him like that, to have seen the look on his face go from suspicious to knocked out, gave her a huge charge.

Gloria was right. She'd been too cautious, too scared to get hurt. Too worried about a future that she couldn't predict.

Even as she watched, congratulating herself on shocking him so completely, the expression in his eyes changed. From stunned to…speculative. He took a halting step closer. He wasn't leaning so heavily on the cane anymore. In fact he didn't use it unless he was going out. "I've been wanting to get you upstairs in that big bed since the first moment I saw you," he told her, lifting a hand and playing with the ends of her hair.

She snorted. "When you first saw me you weren't too happy. You tried to kick me out of the house."

"That's true. Doesn't mean I didn't want you in my bed. A man can think two things at once, you know." He traced his index finger up the line of her hair, sending shivers up and down her body. "Especially if one of them is about sex."

He moved closer and she loved the feel of his

warmth, his personal space meshing with hers so you didn't know where one left off and the other began.

"Why the change of heart?" he wanted to know.

"The truth?"

"Of course."

If she was going to sleep with the man she ought to at least be able to tell him why, after informing him she wouldn't be kissing him anymore she was suddenly planning to become as intimate as two people can be. "I can't stop thinking about it," she said softly, shrugging. "It's getting in the way of my work. I'm usually not a daydreamer. I'm very efficient."

"I've noticed."

"I feel like if we just do it already I'll stop thinking about it."

"Such a romantic."

He'd think she was a complete die-hard romantic if he knew how much her fantasies revolved around that big four-poster. Ever since she'd first seen him stretched out all scruffy and gorgeous she'd associated him with the bed, and adding the two together equaled hot sex in her mind. Maybe she was being stupid, as she accused herself about six times a day, but the truth was she couldn't keep wasting time dreaming about having sex with the man. She'd be better to do it.

Why not? As Gloria had reminded her, she and Rob were both single, and she was young and healthy with a normal sex drive. Nobody was going to get hurt. Why shouldn't they indulge?

His mouth drew closer to hers and, as she lifted her face to his as though compelled, she retained enough sense to say, "I have some rules."

The forward motion stopped.

The sexual intensity in his glance dissipated replaced

by a glint of humor. "Of course you do," he said. "Do I need to go wash my hands first? Change the bedding? Brush my teeth?"

"No." She laughed. "Well, brushing your teeth is probably a good idea. I'll brush mine, too."

"You're a head case, you know that, right?"

"I wasn't going to say any of those things. I was thinking of setting some ground rules."

"Darling, the rules of sex are simple. Nobody gets hurt, and everybody has a good time." He stepped even closer. "And I will make damn sure you have a good time."

Warmth was stealing over her. He might be half joking, but the other half was dead serious. She had a strong feeling that this man would be generous in bed, making sure his partner had at least as much fun as he did.

"That's not— I mean, I'm sure you will but…" She shook her head. "Oh, this is ridiculous. The only rule I wanted to suggest is that we are very clear—this is one night only."

He seemed completely taken aback. "One night only?"

"Yes."

"But we'll barely get started."

"Well, I've thought about it, and that's all I want."

"I don't know." He scratched his cheek where stubble had formed. "I don't do my best work under pressure."

She glanced significantly at his injured leg. "Your profession is all about performing under pressure. I saw the pictures you took in Africa. During the gun battle when you got hurt. They're amazing."

"Thanks. But this is different"

What she didn't tell him was how she'd practically

trembled imagining him in that war zone in constant danger. She could never lose her heart to a man like that. She had to be so careful. Maybe she was stupid even to consider sleeping with him once, but she was suddenly tired of living so rigidly by her rules. Besides, her rules were designed for maximum efficiency of her time. If she was losing sleep having twitchy, hot fantasies about Rob, wouldn't it be easier just to sleep with the guy and be done with it? Then she could put her fantasies behind her.

He wasn't playing according to her program, however. He gazed at her as though she might be more than a little crazy. "I don't know. I've never been the type for one-night stands." He paused, "Well, not since college. I think I'd feel used."

She burst out laughing. "I'm not using you."

"A deal for one night of sex? Even if I want more? What would you call it?"

"I guess I thought we'd be giving each other pleasure for a night. Not that anyone was using anyone else."

"I don't see it that way." He took a step back. "This is probably a bad idea. I'm not at my best mentally or physically right now."

Her astonishment at being turned down by a man for uncomplicated, no-strings-attached sex evaporated when she searched his face and saw real hesitance there. He wasn't playing a game. And then suddenly his behavior made perfect sense.

All his bluster about feeling used, and his earlier comments about everything working properly came back to her.

He was worried about his performance. His leg was far from healed which meant they'd have to make some adjustments. Maybe he wasn't as certain everything was working as he'd told her he was.

He probably thought she was playing games when all she was trying to do was protect her heart. Maybe if she was contemplating being intimate with her body, she should at least let the man into some of what was going on in her head.

"Rob," she began, then didn't know where to go from there. "Rob. You are the sexiest, most interesting man I've met in a really long time."

He didn't appear to be over-the-moon flattered. He simply stood there and listened. She supposed it came from being a journalist. Listening was a skill and not jumping into speech kept the other person talking. As she knew well from her own profession. People often thought they wanted a certain kind of property but sometimes when she listened and encouraged them to talk a different vision would emerge. Not what they thought they wanted, but what would make them happy.

Now he was looking at her and she was going to tell him more than she'd intended. "The thing is I've got a busy career and I'm so focused. I don't want to be distracted by a relationship."

He shook his head. "Who said anything about a relationship? All I said was I'm not a big fan of one-night stands. I'm too old for that crap. I'd have thought you were, too."

"I am. I don't normally indulge like that either. But. Oh, this is so hard. I have this little problem where I... get involved with men I've been intimate with. I don't want to fall for you and then have you break my heart when you go back to war zones and put your life in danger again. So I need to balance the wanting to sleep with you against the fear of losing you. And the only way

I can reconcile the two things is to go into this with a very short-term goal."

"One night."

"Yes."

"That's the craziest damn thing I've ever heard."

She was more let down than she'd have believed possible. She'd really wanted to have one night with him, one night of memories she could enjoy without risking her foolish heart. "So you won't do it?"

He glared at her. "Of course I'll do it. I'm a man. I haven't had a woman in months. You're always underfoot smelling good and looking good. Yeah, I'll take the deal. But I don't like it."

She smiled at the grumpiness in his tone. And in relief. "I understand." She took a deep breath feeling a little shaky now they'd made the decision.

She pulled her electronic organizer out and clicked to her Week at a Glance. "Okay. When do you want to do this?"

A large and very masculine hand reached out and, before she guessed his intent, grabbed the organizer out of her grasp and set it ungently on the table. "How about now?"

"Now? But I was going to bring my nightdress and things over."

"You won't need a nightdress," he informed her stepping closer.

10

"I— OH," AND THAT WAS the last sound Hailey made for a long, long time, as his mouth closed over hers and he reminded her of all the reasons she'd been thinking lustful thoughts of him ever since they'd kissed in the bedroom.

It was different now. She had no frustrations about doing this. She'd made her deal, set boundaries she could live with.

Tonight he'd be her lover.

Tomorrow he'd be back to being her client.

It was fine. It was good. Oh, and the deeper he took the kiss, the more she knew how much she wanted him. She felt herself bending to him, melting against his body as he ran his hands up and down her back, stroking, enticing. His mouth toyed with her, seduced her.

He took her hand and led her up the stairs. He didn't take the cane but held the banister with one hand, and with the other, linked his fingers with hers. She felt the warmth traveling back and forth between their joined hands, felt her heart begin to hammer in anticipation.

She slowed her steps to keep pace with him even though she wanted to race up the stairs and dive into bed.

Get 2 Books FREE!

Harlequin® Books,
publisher of women's fiction,
presents

 Harlequin®

GET 2 BOOKS

We'd like to send you two *Harlequin® Blaze®*
novels absolutely free. Accepting them puts you under
no obligation to purchase any more books.

HOW TO GET YOUR
2 FREE BOOKS AND 2 FREE GIFTS

1. Return the reply card today, and we'll send you two
   Harlequin Blaze novels, absolutely free! We'll even pay
   the postage!

2. Accepting free books places you under no obligation
   to buy anything, ever. Whatever you decide, the free
   books and gifts are yours to keep, free!

3. We hope that after receiving your free books you'll
   want to remain a subscriber, but the choice is yours–
   to continue or cancel, any time at all!

EXTRA BONUS

You'll also get two free mystery gifts!
(worth about $10)

FREE!

Return this card today to get
2 FREE BOOKS and 2 FREE GIFTS!

Harlequin® *Blaze*™

YES! Please send me 2 FREE *Harlequin® Blaze®* novels,
and 2 FREE mystery gifts as well. I understand
I am under no obligation to purchase anything,
as explained on the back of this insert.

151/351 HDL FMJ6

Please Print

FIRST NAME

LAST NAME

ADDRESS

APT.#

CITY

STATE/PROV.

ZIP/POSTAL CODE

Visit us at:
www.ReaderService.com

◄ DETACH AND MAIL CARD TODAY!

When they got to the top of the stairs and he tugged her toward the big bedroom she paused.

"What?" he demanded.

"I keep a toothbrush in the other bathroom," she admitted.

"Of course you do."

"Do you mind if I—"

"Five minutes. If you're not in my bed in five minutes the deal's off."

A little thrill went through her at his macho, caveman attitude.

"I'll be quick," she promised and scooted over to the other bathroom.

She brushed her teeth in record time, astonished, when she saw her face in the mirror, at how a little sexual buzz added color to her cheeks and a sparkle to her eyes. She managed to run a brush through her hair and grab a couple of the condoms she'd also stashed up here when she first started thinking thoughts that had nothing to do with buyers, sellers or amortization schedules.

She dashed down the hall and entered the master suite well within her allotted five minutes.

He came out of the master bathroom and stood in the middle of the room, watching her. The expression in his eyes brought a delicious heaviness to her limbs. With languorous steps, she walked to him, put her arms around his neck and kissed him.

She smiled against his lips, tasting fresh mint. "You brushed your teeth, too."

"Figured I'd get kicked out of bed if I didn't," he grumbled. Then took over the kiss, licking into her mouth, drawing her body against his so she could feel the full force of his passion.

Oh, my.

He raised his head. "Come on."

"Where are we going?" she asked when he took her hand and led her out of the master suite.

"My old room. I feel like I'd get in trouble if I had sex in my grandmother's bed."

"But your bed's a single."

"I know. I wouldn't feel comfortable is all."

"Okay." She tried to be understanding. Of course, grief did strange things to a person, and she respected his feelings, but she loved that four-poster. It was a bed for fantasies and she did not for one moment believe that Mrs. Neeson would begrudge her grandson pleasure. All the same he had to work through his loss in his own way so she went with him to his old bedroom, staged to sell but still containing only a single bed.

When they entered the room, she flipped on the bedside lamp and turned back the coverlet on the ridiculously small bed. "Did you sneak girls up here when you were a teenager?" she asked.

"Truth is I snuck them downstairs to my man cave in the basement." He shot her a wicked look. "I still remember my moves down there if you want to give it a try."

"I am not going down two flights of stairs. And neither are you."

"Maybe later."

She raised her brows at him.

"We've got all night. Don't think you're going to sleep for one minute of it."

A tiny moan started in her throat and almost escaped. She bit it back in the nick of time. How did he do this to her? Driving her wild with no more than a promise of an action-filled night.

She was so hot she needed action now. When she

glanced up at him she got the strong impression he felt the same. He stepped closer and began kissing her again. He wasn't one for wandering all over the place, planting kisses on her cheeks and forehead and any old place his lips felt like landing. He seemed to be a man who liked deep, wet, hungry soul kisses. Which was fine with her. Their bodies strained together as the kiss grew more urgent.

She reached for the buttons of his shirt and began to undo them.

His skin was tanned, the hair on his chest wiry. His collarbones had to be kissed as they were prominent and demanded attention. Then the V where they met and dipped had to be kissed. His skin was warm and silky smooth for a guy who lived such a rugged life. The contrast of smooth skin covered with rough hair delighted her and she had to get the rest of his shirt off so she could play.

This was such a great idea. Play. Nothing serious. No future, just the fun of a sexy man to enjoy for a night before he wandered out of her life again and became no more than a fond memory. What could be better?

When she started tugging the shirt out of the waistband of his jeans, he took over, stripping it off quickly, balling it and chucking it into a corner. Next those big hands went to work on her shirt but he was so clumsy with the tiny buttons that she took over the job, taking her time, making a little striptease out of divesting herself of her top. No matter how passionate she felt she'd never toss her clothing on the floor so she took the extra few seconds to lay the garment neatly over the chair.

"That is a very sexy bra you're wearing," he said.

"Thank you." It was freshly purchased and she'd paid

an outrageous sum for a concoction of pale green silk, lace and underwire.

He lounged against the bed in jeans, bare feet, bare torso. Crossed his arms, showing off impressive biceps. "If I took it off I'd only throw it on the floor so you'd better do it."

The warmth and humor in his tone couldn't disguise the raw hunger beneath. The combination had her catching her breath. If she'd ever been this hungry for a man, she couldn't remember it. She licked her lips, glanced up at him from under her lashes and took her sweet time removing the bra. The way his gaze remained riveted, his breathing grew labored and his hands twitched, she saw she'd spent her money wisely.

When she slowly began to ease the bra down her breasts, feeling the slide of the fabric tease her nipples, he said, "I'm not sure I'm going to survive the night."

She grinned at him. "What a way to go."

She wasn't one to flaunt her body but he was so obviously enjoying her little show and his enjoyment only added to hers so she revealed her breasts slowly, taking his grunt as a sign of approval, then laid the bra over the back of the chair. With her back to him, she undid her skirt and wiggled the thing off her, giving him an enticing view of the matching thong panties, and the thigh-high stockings that weren't very comfortable but that made up in sexiness what they lacked in comfort.

"Who'd have thought," he said softly, "that under all that crisp business clothing, you were hiding that underwear. And that body."

Before she could turn around, his hands were on her waist and he was kissing the back of her neck, running his palms up her belly to cup her breasts. His palms were warm and a little rough, which felt delicious on her tender skin.

She felt the bulge of his arousal in his jeans as he bumped up against her and the feel of this denim-covered hot man rubbing against her near-nakedness had her turning to embrace him.

The jeans hung low on his hips, his long torso was tawny, sprinkled with sun freckles on his broad shoulders. He felt so solid that she leaned into him, rubbing herself against him shamelessly.

He stumbled.

Her big, strong, sexy guy stumbled and barely bit back a wince of pain.

Her hand flew to her mouth. "Oh, I'm so sorry. I forgot your leg. Did I hurt you?"

"No. Just got unbalanced," he replied gruffly.

She could have kicked herself for being so thoughtless. She knew better, though, than to make an issue of it. Instead she walked to the bed, knowing he'd follow her, and sat. When he came toward her, she leaned forward and kissed his belly where a line of hair arrowed into his waistband and then she tackled the fly.

She eased the zipper over the enticing bulge and began to ease the jeans down over his hips.

And soon realized he'd gone skimpier on the undies than she had.

He wasn't wearing any.

Staring back at her was the nicest cock she'd ever seen. Long and thick and standing proud. As she continued to stare, her hands halted as though frozen, she could have sworn it stood even straighter to attention, as though proud to have stunned her so thoroughly.

She couldn't stop herself; she had to touch it. Wrapping her hand around the hardness, she squeezed gently and heard him pull in his breath. "Remember, it's been a while for me. Don't want to embarrass myself," he said through gritted teeth.

"Right." She quickly let go and continued removing his pants. When she saw his thigh wound she had to bite back a gasp. She'd expected, if she'd thought about it at all, that the spot would be neatly bandaged. It wasn't.

The bullet had blasted a hole in the front of his thigh and another out the back. It was roughly stitched, but still red and raw-looking. "That looks so painful," she said, unable to help herself.

"I should have covered it up," he said. "Didn't know this was going to happen."

"No. It's okay. I'm only sorry this happened to you."

Now that she understood the mess his leg was in, she understood that she was going to have to be careful not to hurt him. Mostly in her experience, especially the first time, she'd let the man take the lead in the bedroom. Tonight she was going to have to take control, if only to stop him from hurting himself.

She kind of liked the idea of taking control, especially knowing it would make his night more pleasurable.

She eased herself off the bed, kneeling before him to continue pulling off his jeans. When he'd stepped out of them she pushed him gently back on the bed until he was half reclining looking up at her quizzically.

"What are you doing?" he asked, half belligerent, half husky.

She smiled at him, channeling every sexy siren who had ever gone before her. "Remember when you used to lie in your single bed in this very room and fantasize about a woman who would come to you and give you everything you desire?"

"Oh, yeah."

"I am your fantasy."

He reached out to cup the back of her head. His voice was husky when he said, "You have no idea."

In truth she wasn't the boldest woman in town but her desire not to hurt him was stronger than her fear of making a fool of herself.

Standing in full view of him she slowly slipped off her thong, enjoying the way his gaze stayed riveted on her every move. She tingled at the intensity of his gaze. And then, slowly, taking care not to bump his bad leg, she put one knee on the bed and straddled him.

"You're a take-charge kind of woman."

"Do you have a problem with that?"

He shook his head, "No."

"Good."

She smiled to herself thinking of all the fantasies she'd had of this moment. They'd taken place in the big bed in the master bedroom, or on the rug in front of the fireplace. And in every one of them, she'd been the one lying at ease while he pleasured her in ways that spoke to her deepest fantasies. Not one of which included her doing all the work.

And yet there was something enormously erotic taking charge. In knowing she had it in her power to give him pleasure. She felt free, powerful, sexy.

Tossing her hair over her shoulder, she leaned down to kiss him deeply, and, as she did, she took hold of his cock and began to rub it back and forth across her clit, bringing her to full enjoyment of the moment and torturing him a little along the way.

She'd never been much for living in the moment. A woman with two organizers tended to spend a lot of her energy on the future and usually Hailey was fine with that. But there were times, like now, when she couldn't do anything but live in the moment. If she looked at the future even as closely as tomorrow, this would all be over. This man lying beneath her, all warm and sexy and naked, wouldn't be her lover anymore. He'd revert to her client.

Clothed.

This feeling of joyful abandon would end. In truth she'd never been one for short-term relationships. They never seemed worth the effort, but to have an affair that was only going to last one night took all the anxiety away. There was no worry about tomorrow or his expectations or her expectations or whether he'd call and whether she wanted him to. There was no tomorrow, which meant there was only glorious perfect now. And as she slipped the condom onto him and sank, slowly, onto his jutting cock, she knew she'd never, ever had a more perfect now.

11
___

HE FILLED HER, made himself at home within her body, and then they began to move together. The connection between them when their gazes met was almost more intimate than their joined bodies. "This," she said, leaning close so she could brush the words against his lips like a kiss, "is a perfect moment."

"Oh, yeah, and it's about to get more perfect."

"Mmm." She'd have said he let her set her own pace except that it felt as though they were in perfect sync, rising and falling together as their bodies surged and ebbed.

His chest was rising and falling with the effort. She wanted to slow things down, to make this wonderful now last forever, but then he slipped a hand between them and began to touch her hot spot.

He'd barely touched her, brushing his fingertips across her clit, when she reared back, climaxing in a burst of heat that felt volcanic. She felt herself squeezing him, watched his blue eyes lose their focus, but still he kept touching her, easily, softly. She felt herself rising again and rode him hard. The bed protested. She didn't care if they broke the bed; she'd buy a new one.

He bucked beneath her, driving up and into her, hitting her G-spot and an entire alphabet of new erogenous zones she hadn't known she possessed.

He grabbed her hips when he came, arching up and taking her with him so her cries echoed his.

Fireworks exploded behind her eyes and for a moment she couldn't catch her breath.

The moment stretched to eternity and back again and then a glorious sense of peace filled her.

"Oh, my goodness," she said, slumping onto his sweat-damp chest, listening to the pounding of his heart. They remained connected intimately because she didn't want to let him go.

They didn't speak, both savoring the experience, enjoying the afterglow.

After a few minutes had passed, she kissed his neck, and wiggled her pelvis. To her surprise, a rock-hard penis still filled her. She lifted her head to look at him. "Didn't you come?"

He snorted. "Ah, yeah. In case you didn't notice, I did."

"But you're still hard." She heard her own puzzlement.

"It's kind of a thing I have," he said, looking vaguely embarrassed.

"What kind of a thing?"

"I can stay hard between sessions."

"You mean you can go again? Right away?"

"Yep."

She'd never heard of such a thing. "Are you, like, multi-orgasmic?"

"Are we going to analyze this or are we going to enjoy it?" he snapped.

She decided to let her actions speak for her and

reached down to cup his scrotum, stroking him. Then she began to play, exploring all the ways they could make love without putting strain on his wounded leg. With the first rush of need taken care of, they were free to take a leisurely pace and simply enjoy each other.

She'd never had so much fun in bed.

Ever.

He was earthy, giving, athletic and possessed stamina unlike anything she'd ever experienced before. She thought she'd be worn-out long before morning.

They dozed, then starving, raided the kitchen at three in the morning.

"What do you want to eat?" she asked, opening the refrigerator. His robe hung on her small frame, while he'd shoved only his jeans on so he was bare of chest and foot. Exactly how she liked him.

"Grilled cheese sandwiches."

"With pickles."

"I'll get the frying pan heating. You get the food."

They sat at the kitchen table munching sandwiches and pickles and drinking milk until they had enough energy to go back upstairs. They curled up together in that ridiculously small bed. As he played idly with her breasts, and she drew silly doodles with her fingers on his belly, they talked.

"How did you get into real estate?" he asked.

"When I was a kid we moved thirteen times in twelve years. My dad was in the army. He loved change and new places." She glanced at him. "Kind of like you."

"I guess."

"When you've never had something you can get pretty obsessed. I never felt like I had a real home." She loved the line of softer hair on his lower belly and she stroked it as she talked. "I mean, I always had a home, but eventually my poor mother just couldn't be bothered to unpack everything. What was the point? We'd only be moving again. We lived in military housing or rentals off base and never decorated or anything." She made a face. "When other kids were reading *Seventeen* magazine I read home-decorating magazines. And TV? I watched *The OC* for the houses, not the cute guys. I used to pretend that Martha Stewart was my mom and I lived in her house with her."

"Did your friends think you were nuts?"

"I didn't have any real friends. I've always envied those lifetime friendships women have. Oh, sure, I got over my shyness, learned to make casual friends and to protect my heart so it didn't break when I had to leave a place and start all over again in another."

He rolled over, cupped her face and kissed her softly. "That sounds so lonely."

"It was, but I also became pretty self-sufficient and independent. Good qualities in a Realtor."

"Where are your parents?" he asked.

"My dad passed away a couple of years ago just before he would have retired. My mom remarried and lives in California. She works in a furniture store and she never goes anywhere if she can help it."

"You feel that way?"

"No, I love to travel. But I want to know I've got a home to come back to. I suppose I have a little of both of my parents in me. I've been in the same rental for four years. I'm saving up to buy a place." She sighed. "I wish I could afford Bellamy House. This is my ideal. A home you could stay in for your whole life. Raise kids. Maybe get a dog. Get to know your neighbors."

"This is the place for that all right."

She was drowsy, so sated from sex that her body felt

limp and well-used. But she didn't want to waste any time sleeping.

It was nice, swapping secrets in the dark. "How about you? I saw a picture of your mother, but you never talk about your parents."

"Not much to tell," he said, staring up at the ceiling. "My parents got divorced when I was young. I never knew my dad. Mom was a hippie. A real free spirit. She had a lot of boyfriends. Usually the guys didn't want a little kid around."

A ball of anger began to form in her belly. Who would do that to a sweet little boy, the kind she was sure Rob would have been?

"She used to send me to my grandmother's for months at a stretch. That suited all of us. Then she'd end up single or miss me and haul me back."

In an odd way, she thought their backgrounds were more alike than she'd realized.

"Everything changed when I was fourteen." He turned, running his hand over her breasts, down her belly. "My mom had a new loser, a real piece of work. I wasn't a little kid anymore and I'd had enough. I hitch-hiked to the Canadian border. Had great plans about working up north on oil rigs. I'd heard you could make a pile of money. The border guards didn't think too much of my plans. I told them my mother was dead so they called my grandmother."

His hand slipped lower and she had to concentrate to hang on to the thread of the story. "She made a deal with me. If I finished school and lived with her she'd buy me a round-the-world ticket for graduation."

"What a smart woman."

"Oh, she was. She didn't yell at me or anything. She

got it. She also let me turn that bathroom downstairs into a darkroom and helped me buy my first camera."

"Wow."

"Could you spread your legs a little wider?"

She was happy to comply.

"After journalism school, when I was twenty-two, I took her up on that ticket. I was in the wrong place at the wrong time. Which for a budding photojournalist was exactly the right place at the right time. I was in Namibia. It was August 1999. The Caprivi Liberation Army claimed that the government was neglecting their region. Guerrillas attacked the Namibian military and police on August second. I'd only been in the region a couple of days. I was one of the first photographers on the scene and got some great footage."

"Wow. Some holiday." Then he moved his fingers and she sighed with pleasure.

"I sent my photos to Gary Wallenberg who was then bureau chief for Africa for *World Week*. Gary snapped them up. I started freelancing and then got hired on permanent staff. Like I said, right place, right time."

And the right talent, she thought.

"What happened to your mom?"

"She died. A few years ago. Cancer."

"I'm sorry."

"Yeah. Me, too. But the funny thing is, I miss my grandmother so much more. I guess in every way that counts, she was my real mother."

He kissed her, and the hand playing with her moved in earnest. Reaching over, she found him hard again. The guy was amazing.

It would soon be daylight, and she didn't plan to waste a minute of the night sleeping.

SHE DIDN'T THINK she'd been asleep but when her cell phone alarm chirped it jerked her awake. From the grittiness of her eyes and the almost light-headed feeling when she sat up, she suspected her night's sleep had been counted in minutes rather than hours.

Rob was instantly awake and sitting up, squinting at the window. Dawn had barely broken.

"What time is it?" he asked sleepily.

"Six-thirty."

"Do you have a meeting or something?"

"No. I need to get home and shower, that's all." In truth, she'd set her alarm deliberately early so she could avoid any morning awkwardness.

He wrapped his arms around her, drawing her back into the warmth of his embrace, his sleep-warmed skin cocooning her. "You could shower here," he said, kissing the back of her shoulders. "I'll wash your back for you."

She was tempted. Yet she knew she'd done the right thing in making such a big deal of only spending one night together. He was too sexy, too wonderful for her not to fall for him. And the last thing she wanted in her life was a wandering man.

She'd promised herself from the time she could understand why they moved all the time that she'd never get involved with a man who didn't stay in one place. By that very simple standard Rob was about the last man she should ever date.

So, reluctantly, she moved away, showed him a smiling face when she turned to him, kissed him once and then resolutely put her feet onto the floor. The hardwood was cold against her bare feet, and as she rose, she shivered. The sooner she got out of here the better.

"Will I see you later?" he asked sleepily.

"I'm not sure," she said in what she hoped was a businesslike tone. "I have a showing here tomorrow. I'll let you know for sure. As for today, unless somebody calls and wants a showing, I probably won't see you."

"You're really serious about this one-night thing, aren't you?" She heard disbelief in his voice. After the astonishing night they'd spent together she could understand how he thought she must be crazy. As she scrambled into her clothes she knew in her heart she'd be crazy to continue. Only pain would result if she ever let herself fall for a man like Rob.

"I have to, Rob. Don't you see? You're a rolling stone." He didn't argue with her, merely nodded slowly, a bleakness in his eyes she didn't want to see.

As she left the room, she said softly to herself, "And I'm moss."

12

Rob scowled at his coffee. It was his third cup of the day and it didn't seem to be doing the usual job of waking him up and energizing him.

After a night like last night he should be skipping and jumping like some guy in a Viagra commercial. Instead he felt the way he had done right after he found out his grandmother was dead. Bereft. As though something vital to his happiness had been ripped from him.

"Get a grip," he snarled to the French press, sitting on the counter with nothing but a sludge of pressed grounds in its glass bottom. That was kind of how he felt. As if someone, namely Hailey, had crushed every last drop of flavor and vitality out of him and left nothing but a squeezed-out lump of sludge behind.

He wasn't big on self-reflection, but for some reason she'd slipped under his skin and made him see himself in a light that wasn't entirely flattering.

Hailey had made it clear that she could never take a man like him seriously.

No. Not a man like him.

Him.

In her view, as a potential mate he didn't cut it. Not

that he wanted to cut it, but it was galling to know that she wouldn't sleep with him again because of that.

And she was right, damn it, he thought savagely as he tossed the dregs of his coffee down the sink. He wasn't mate material. Not for a woman like her, with plans for the future—and husband, kids and a family van written all over her. Probably he was irked simply because she'd decreed there'd be no more sex.

He thought of that sweet body convulsing around him, of the intensity of their night together, and he thought it was a crime, a class-B felony at least, to deny both of them pleasure like that simply because he wasn't a stay-at-home kind of guy.

Well, he wasn't a stay-at-home guy. The reason he was brooding, he suspected, was because he was bored and that made him twitchy. He needed to get back to work where he belonged and out of Fremont where he so clearly didn't.

He hobbled upstairs to his grandmother's bedroom and put on athletic shorts, sneakers and a workout shirt.

He'd been here for four weeks already. It was time he quit lounging and started working out. Once geared up, he headed out to the local running track. *A mile in six.* Trust Gary to punish him while he was on leave.

When he got to the track, there were only three other joggers. An overweight middle-aged woman shuffling along with earbuds hanging and two younger women who were chatting as they ran.

He started slowly, walking once around the track, trying to pretend there was no pain in his left thigh. Even though Hailey had—in her own sweet way—tried to keep from hurting him there was no way a man could have athletic sex and not use his thigh muscles. So he was sore.

Big deal. It had been so worth it.

He broke into a jog. Making almost a circuit of the track before sweat broke out on his brow and his leg felt as if shards of glass were being shoved into his thigh each time his foot hit the ground.

The obese woman passed him, huffing and wheezing, but outpacing him.

He made it another half a circuit by sheer grit before limping off the field cursing all the way home.

"WHAT THE HELL DID YOU DO?" Doc Greene demanded to know when he showed up for his appointment—an appointment it had almost killed him to make.

"I went jogging."

"Are you insane? It's been four weeks. I told you no running before six weeks."

"I'm a fast healer." He scowled. "Look, I lost the scrip for painkillers you gave me." He'd chucked it out but he didn't feel like sharing that information. "I need a new one, that's all."

Doc Greene glared at him from over his bifocals. "This injury involves an eight- to ten-week recovery. You are not in the condition to run."

Rob gritted his teeth. "I need to run a mile in six minutes before my boss will take me back."

"Pushing it too soon will only hold you back."

"There must be something I can do."

"What you want is physiotherapy."

It just got worse and worse. "Physiotherapy? I didn't put my back out. I got shot."

"I know. And your muscles need rebuilding. A good physio can get you back on the road sooner than you will by running yourself into the ground."

Rob couldn't describe the turmoil swirling around

his gut. He didn't mean to speak, yet he blurted, "I need to get out of this town."

"Why?" Doc gave him a penetrating look that made him feel as though he should be reclining on a couch reciting all the ills done to him in childhood.

He wasn't going to tell a septuagenarian doctor that a confusing mix of hot sex and no future with one stunning Realtor was driving him away so he said, "I don't belong here."

"Of course you do. You've lived most of your life here. People are proud of you. And you're the only living connection with your grandmother. She wanted you to stay. Why do you think she left you the house? It's not like you need the money with that fancy job of yours."

He'd never even thought about why Gran had left him Bellamy House. He'd assumed it was because he was her closest relative.

"What if I don't want to stay? What if I can't?"

"There are charities your grandmother supported who would love to get that house."

A light bulb went on inside his head. He wasn't rich, as Doc Greene seemed to be suggesting, but he did fine. Maybe that's what he'd do. Give the place to some deserving charity his grandmother had supported. That would take away this weird feeling he had that he had to choose the next owners, that the property should go to someone his grandmother would have approved of. If he gave the place away it would also sever his relationship with Hailey. He'd make sure she still got her commission for the sale. He owed her that. However, if he gifted the property to charity, he wouldn't be forced to see Hailey several times a week and relive their single night together like a particularly hot erotic movie that looped endlessly in his head.

Doc scribbled on a pad, ripped it off and handed him the page. "That's for the painkillers." Then he scribbled on another page. "And that's for a physio who is also a personal trainer. She'll get you doing your mile in six." He gave him a sharp look. "When your body is ready."

"Thanks, Doc."

He limped out. While he waited for his prescription to be filled downstairs in the pharmacy he noticed that the latest issue of *World Week* was on the stands.

He bought it along with the pills. Not wanting to go home, he headed to the friendly café down the road. Maybe a professional could brew him a coffee that would taste better than what he'd made himself this morning.

When he entered Beananza he had the place almost to himself. He'd missed the lunch rush and whatever rush was next hadn't started yet. He ordered an Americano.

"You're the guy who inherited Bellamy House," the barista said.

"That's right."

The guy wore a shirt that read Grounds for Divorce, and featured a cartoon of a woman in a business suit pouring coffee from a pot that was empty, while her suit-clad spouse sipped from a full mug.

"Why is it always the guys who are depicted as selfish morons?" He wondered aloud, pointing at the shirt.

The barista looked down as though he didn't remember what shirt he'd put on that morning. "Maybe because they so often are."

He grunted. He'd like to get a shirt that said Men Should Stand Up for Each Other!

"Hailey and Julia are both friends of mine," the guy

in the offensive shirt added. "They sure have been thrilled about showcasing that house."

"They've done a great job," Rob said. Because they had. Hailey had also done a great job messing with his head and ruining his day. That, however, was nobody's business but his.

He took his coffee to a spot where he felt he'd be least likely to be disturbed. After popping a couple of the pain pills, he opened *World Week.*

Things were heating up in a Baltic state, one he'd been to before and knew well. The photographer Gary had sent had done an okay job, but he knew he could have done better.

The knowledge irked.

Famine in Africa. And the same obvious photos. The same tired stories. He was convinced he could have found something fresh in this latest heart-wrenching human tragedy.

Disasters were occurring all over the world and other people were reporting it, other cameras were capturing it. He felt like banging his mug down on the counter in frustration.

He flipped through the domestic news. Politics, more home foreclosures, the religious right—some days he wanted to crawl under the Aurora Bridge and live with the troll.

He left the magazine on the counter and went home. His cell phone rang. He saw it was Hailey and in his eagerness to answer he fumbled the phone. His bad mood and the pain in his leg vanished.

"Hi," he said. "And yes, I'm free tonight."

There was a tiny pause.

"Hello, Rob. I've got a new client who is very interested in Bellamy House. I'd like to bring him around tomorrow around eleven."

Okay, she was putting on her professional act and he got it. She'd done the same this morning though she hadn't seemed quite so professional when she was naked. Still, with every article of clothing she'd donned he'd felt the warm, passionate lover easing away from him and Hailey the Realtor taking her place.

Well? He'd taken the deal, hadn't he? Agreed to just one night. How could he have imagined that one perfect night could mess with him so badly? And now he had to see her on a regular basis? Pretend they were only business acquaintances?

He couldn't do it. He'd find a worthy charity to take the house. And then he'd leave. So, he couldn't run a mile in six. Or sixty the way he felt. But he could convalesce in a hundred different places around the globe, not one of which was full of memories. And where there'd be no Hailey making him feel that he wasn't enough of a man for her.

He made himself focus on the conversation.

"Him? A single guy? What does a single guy want with Bellamy House?"

"Maybe he's planning to settle down and have a family," she said, all neutral, as though she weren't sticking a knife into him.

"Eleven is fine," he said. He didn't like the sound of a single guy buying the property. He'd give Bellamy House to a charity first. He wasn't about to share that with Hailey just yet. He needed to do some research first.

He also didn't like the tone she'd used with him. Oh, it was professional and friendly enough. That was exactly the problem. He didn't want professional and friendly. He wanted sexy and intimate. She'd warned him up front how it would be; all the same it hurt to go from client to lover and back again within twelve hours. In fact it sucked.

He said goodbye, and, for the first time since they'd started working together, he determined to be far away from his own house for tomorrow's showing.

He'd thought his day couldn't get any worse, his mood any blacker when his cell phone rang again. He didn't recognize the local number.

"Robert Klassen?" a cool female voice inquired.

"Yes." Nobody called him Robert unless they were trying to sell him something and whatever it was, he wasn't buying.

"This is Keystone Funeral Home calling—"

"Thanks anyway but I don't plan to die for a while."

Weren't there enough deaths in the world? Did they have to troll for business among the young and healthy? He looked at his leg. Maybe this was targeted marketing after all.

"Mr. Klassen, I'm calling about Agnes Neeson. Your grandmother, I believe."

"Oh." Funeral home. Gran. He hated thinking of them together. He needed to end this call. "Didn't your bill get paid? Her lawyer took care of all the bills."

"Yes, payment was received. We've got her ashes. Mr. Klassen, you can come by anytime during office hours to pick them up."

"Her ashes? My grandmother's ashes?" He knew there'd been a celebration of her life shortly after she died. He'd never thought there were ashes somewhere waiting for a home. "What am I supposed to do with them?"

"Whatever you'd like, sir. We do have a memorial

field. Your grandmother's ashes would be buried under a tasteful plaque. We'd be happy to discuss placing your loved one in our memorial garden at your leisure."

A plaque in a field? He couldn't imagine anything worse. His grandmother wasn't going to end up in the middle of a lawn in a row of similar plaques, the last resting place of those with no imagination or a family who couldn't be bothered to scatter the ashes somewhere meaningful.

"Thanks. I'll pick them up."

His first instinct was to call Hailey and talk to her about the ashes. How had she done this to him? Turned him from an independent man who made his own decisions to someone who wanted to ask her where he should put his grandmother's remains? A woman she'd never even met?

The bizarre thing was that he was certain she'd have the right idea.

13

JULIA SPENT A MISERABLE evening deleting every single one of the emails from the guy she now referred to as her scammer.

Inevitably she couldn't simply delete the emails, not without reading each message over again. Nor could she put his photos in her computer's trash bin, not without gazing longingly at the man she'd believed was writing to her.

In the time since she'd discovered she'd been scammed she'd done research on the internet, something she should have done earlier, and learned there was an entire industry based on men creating fake personas to lure unwary women—such as herself—into sending them money.

The horror stories she'd read had practically made her hair stand up. Women had sold jewelry, antiques and family heirlooms to send more and more money to these men who professed love and made promises for the future if only they could send another thousand dollars for airfare or five thousand to pay for urgent medical attention—or some other bogus reason.

Once they'd taken the initial bait these women often

went into debt to keep their dream alive. It was ludicrous, these seemingly rational women sending their life savings off to men who didn't exist. How could they be so stupid? Now she knew.

Julia understood two things. One: there is no escaping the foolishness a woman will stoop to if she believes she's in love. And two: she, Julia, had to accept she wasn't as smart as she thought she was.

She knew in her deepest heart that there'd been a moment when she'd actually considered sending him the money, so deeply had she bought into the fantasy of him and of them together. That's probably what made her the maddest, knowing she'd been manipulated in the most humiliating manner and by someone who operated on the other side of the world and was virtually untouchable. All she could do was report her story to the internet dating site and admit to being one more fool for love.

Even as she accepted that she was a dupe, still she reread all the emails. Now that she knew the truth, she could see there was a certain generic tone to them. He'd been awfully quick to profess his affection for someone he'd never met.

And, gritting her teeth, she realized she'd been even quicker to accept his professions as genuine.

And those photos!

The guy whose pictures were so hot she worried he would be too good-looking for her, they were photos of a model, the likeness stolen and used to lure her.

She knew she should rip the Band-Aid off, chuck the emails and the photos and empty her computer's trash bin.

She knew that.

Still, she tortured herself going through it all again. It

was like looking at photos of a great vacation or studying pictures of someone you've loved who's died. That's how she felt. She experienced the bittersweet sadness of remembering past happiness. Because she had been happy. She'd already written the story in her head. Their first date, the first kiss.

How many idle moments had she spent wondering when they'd first make love and where it would happen?

Fool!

After wallowing in her own misery for as long as she could stand, she did what had to be done. Deleted the emails and the photos into the trash. Purged the guy from her life. Or the fantasy out of her life.

It was early evening, and she felt twitchy and out of sorts. Maybe just to torture herself more, she logged on to the dating site and checked to see if anyone had tried to contact her. She had an email from a guy who appeared to have spread his net pretty wide since his home address was in Portland, Oregon, and she had no interest in a long-distance relationship. She'd just had one with a Nigerian and that hadn't gone so well.

She deleted Mr. Portland. And noticed the initial message from John was still in her dating-site inbox. She clicked on his profile, which was still active.

John wasn't romantic or exciting; she'd never worry that he was too good-looking for her and he didn't make her nervous with trying to make a good impression. He was a nice man who was alone and she was a nice woman who was alone. Maybe she should take him up on his offer of dinner or a movie. Anything to get out of her apartment and out of her own head.

Before she could talk herself out of what was probably a truly terrible idea, she'd dug out his card and called him. He answered right away. After she identified herself she didn't know what to say next. She fumbled around a bit and then said, "I'm having a lousy day. I was wondering if you'd like to go out and get some dinner with me? Or a drink or something."

There was a pause on his end and she closed her eyes, wishing she'd never dreamed up this stupid idea. What if he said no? Could she stand being rejected by somebody she wasn't even interested in?

Then he said, "I'm finishing something up. I could be free in an hour. Would that work for you?"

She was so relieved she said, "Oh, thank you."

He chuckled, but in an understanding way. "Day was that bad, huh? You like sushi?"

"Love it."

"You know Sushi Master?"

"I've never been there but I'll find it."

He gave her quick directions, then said, "Great. I'll meet you there at eight."

"Looking forward to it." When she hung up she found, to her surprise, that she was.

Since John was nice enough to accept a pity date with her she vowed not to be late. She was leaving her apartment only a few minutes after she'd planned to when she passed her computer. She took a step past it toward the door, then stopped.

"Do it!" she commanded herself out loud.

Without giving herself time for any foolish last thoughts, she emptied her trash and turned off her computer. A tiny pang of grief hit her when she knew the photos, emails and the dreams she'd spun around them, were gone forever.

AFTER SHE PARKED, she headed into the restaurant a respectable five minutes late. John was already sitting at a table, a beer in front of him. "You were early," she complained, when she settled herself across from him.

"No. You were late."

"Five minutes? That's on time in my books."

He shook his head. "How many planes have you missed?"

She made a big production of picking up the menu and opening it. A vast selection of rolls and sashimi and platters met her eyes. "What's good here?"

A waitress appeared. "Would you like something to drink?"

"Vodka tonic," she said, and then realized she didn't need to be on a diet anymore. She didn't plan to get naked with the cute blond guy since the closest she'd ever get to him would be seeing him on a billboard or a magazine ad somewhere. Thus, her caloric intake was her business. "No. Wait. I'll have a beer also." She gestured to his glass. "Whatever he's having."

"Sapporo?"

"Perfect."

Then she closed her menu. "Why don't we get a plate of assorted sushi and go wild."

"Sounds good to me."

She glanced around and found the decor to be pretty standard, but clean and full of clients, many of them Asian, on a Tuesday night, which suggested the food was particularly good.

John's hair hung over his forehead in a straight bang as though his mother had cut it using a bowl. His shirt was old, out of date and too short in the sleeves.

But he was here. And she was grateful.

"So, you had a lousy day."

"I did.'

There was a pause.

"Anything you want to talk about?"

"No."

"Okay."

There was another pause. She tried to think of something to talk about that was neutral and didn't involve the weather, which would be pathetic. She got the sense he was doing the same thing.

She let out a breath. "I did an unbelievably stupid thing, and I didn't want to be alone tonight to brood."

"Hey, don't beat yourself up. We all do stupid things."

"I never thought I'd be the kind of person to fall for... Oh, heck, I might as well just tell you." And so she did.

The whole sad, sorry tale.

"I'm sorry," he said when she'd finished her story.

"That's all you have to say?"

"What do you want me to say?"

"I don't know. Make me feel better, I guess."

Their sushi platter arrived and he gestured to her to go first. She chose a California roll.

He went for the salmon, handling his chopsticks like a pro. He might dress like a goof but at least he could go out for sushi without making a fool of himself.

He certainly liked his wasabi, she noticed, as she watched him eat his roll. When he'd finished chewing and swallowed, he sat back and regarded her. "I think a lot of people go into online dating thinking they're going to meet the perfect partner. Maybe, though, there isn't a perfect partner. Maybe we need to be more open to trying new people, to thinking that it's okay to settle for someone you like who can fulfill a few of your needs without some romantic notion that there's a perfect match out there."

"You're saying that I bought into a fantasy."

"Absolutely. Romantic movies and Valentine's Day

cards, all kinds of fiction revolves around the idea that there's a missing half of us. That we'll find that other person and wow, fireworks! We'll be happy forever-more." He chose a dynamite roll. "It's so bogus."

"What if it isn't bogus? What if there is a perfect match?"

He stared at her, his food halfway to his mouth. "You can't still believe that?"

"I don't know," she said, kind of embarrassed. "I want to believe it. In spite of all that's happened. In spite of the fact that I'm…not as young as I used to be, I still believe there's a perfect someone out there for me. Don't you?"

"No, I don't. I think that all you can hope for is not to be lonely. At least some of the time."

"That's so depressing."

He shrugged. "I think of it as realistic."

"Let's get realistic. Tell me about your dating suc-cess. It's got to be so much easier being a man. There are so many more women in Seattle, you must have your pick of nice ones."

"Oh, you'd be surprised." He grabbed a piece of pick-led ginger deftly with chopsticks. Then glanced up at her. "Do you really want to hear this?"

"Yes. I do. I think we both know there wasn't any chemistry between us. I like the idea of having a male friend I can talk to about this stuff."

"It seems strange."

"After what I told you, nothing you could say would shock me. Really."

"Well, I wasn't scammed, at least not so far. So I suppose that's positive. Otherwise, online dating has been a pretty dismal experience."

She thought of the way she'd ditched him so quickly.

Realized that he was a really nice man. What he needed most was a makeover.

Or someone who could see past the bad hair, the worse clothes, the outdated glasses.

She really hoped there was a nice woman out there for John. He deserved her.

14

ONE NIGHT WASN'T SUPPOSED to change your life, Rob thought, annoyed. Or who you were.

It was ridiculous.

Sexual frustration, that's all he was feeling, and the weird notion that he'd been somehow rejected before he'd even got started.

If Hailey wanted to deprive them both of a satisfying few weeks of great sex while he was in town, that was her business.

One thing he knew was that he wasn't planning to be around when she had her showing today. Nope. He didn't want to experience the impact of those blue-gray eyes and remember how they'd softened to molten silver when she grew aroused or see her decked out in one of her fancy suits and know exactly what she looked like—felt like—without a stitch on.

He wasn't interested in torturing himself.

He was going to be long gone before the single dude showed up to look at his house. He didn't want to meet the guy and he didn't want to see Hailey. Not when she was treating him as though they'd never been any closer to each other than shaking hands.

He had enough problems, like a physiotherapist now added to the retinue of annoying women in his life, and then there was the box on top of his desk containing his grandmother's ashes. He had to figure out what to do with them. What she'd have wanted. Why could the woman not have left instruction in her will? Why leave it to him?

Women. He couldn't believe they could be almost as aggravating dead as were alive.

Still, it gave him an odd sense of peace to work on his project with that box in the corner. He hadn't gone so far as to talk to his dead gran though he'd stopped himself just in time not an hour ago. He needed to find her a better resting place.

The day was mild and the park across the street seemed like a great place to read the newspaper and have his camera handy for all the little dramas that might unfold. A little before eleven o'clock, Hailey drew up and got out of her car, one of the feature sheets she'd created for Bellamy House in her hand, along with the briefcase she carried around with her. Even from here he was struck by her beauty. A ray of sunlight caught her hair, lighting it gold. She was wearing a skirt and a suit jacket and heels that showed off the slim line of her legs.

He was overcome by the rushing sensation of recalling the feel of those legs gripping him as she rode him. He grew instantly hard at the memory and was thankful to have the *Seattle Times* as a shield. He vowed then and there that he and his hot Realtor were going to have a rematch. No way was that a one-night thing.

A second car drew up behind hers, a navy luxury sedan with rental plates. He watched a tall clean-cut guy wearing jeans and a sports jacket emerge from the vehicle. Hailey went toward him with her hand outstretched.

Watching him grasp Hailey's hand for way too long brought out a gut-deep urge in Rob to plow his fist into the guy's face.

Except he had no right. Scowling, he lifted the telephoto and focused in for a closer look.

Since the weather was nice, Hailey spent a few minutes pointing out the exterior features, no doubt giving a little of the house's history and describing the neighborhood.

The client nodded, asking a few questions.

Slick. That was the word that went through Rob's mind as he took him in. Salesman type. Clean-shaven, expensive haircut, slight tan in a face that had once probably been termed boyishly handsome. He looked to be maybe forty. Rob didn't wear expensive clothes, thought it was a pretentious waste of money, but he'd learned to assess a man's clothing. Where it was from, how much it had cost. It was part of his job.

He might not be able to name the designer, but he knew that jacket was made by one. British at a guess, worn over a black T-shirt. The loafers were Italian and so shiny you wondered if the guy walked anywhere. The jeans were from the good old U.S.A. The kind fools spent three hundred bucks for. The guy barely looked at the feature sheet in his manicured hand. All his attention was on Hailey. Rob didn't like it. Not one bit.

He'd seen enough. He started to pack up his camera, still keeping the couple across the street in view. A moving truck lumbered by, obscuring them momentarily from view. Traffic was light. A few cars drove by. A school bus, and no doubt Hailey took that opportunity to mention the excellent schools in the area. Even though the man didn't have kids.

A cop car came down the street. Mr. Slick turned quickly away so he had his back to the street when the cruiser drove by.

A million people would have seen that gesture and thought nothing of it. Those people hadn't been where Rob had been, hadn't seen the things he'd seen. As though covering his abrupt reaction to seeing a police car, Mr. Slick then pointed to the foundation of the house. Hailey walked closer to him and seemed to be answering questions. Rob swiftly raised the camera once more.

All he needed was… Yes, Mr. Slick turned to glance up the street and down again. Looking for more cop cars?

Luckily, the man didn't pay any attention to what was going on in the park. Rob shot off a few photos, with no clear idea why.

Then the Realtor and her client entered Bellamy House.

Now what?

Limp into the house and confront the guy? Threaten a complete stranger with his grandmother's cane?

Even though he felt an urge to do something stupid and dramatic, common sense told him that the man wasn't here to harm Hailey. For some reason he was interested in real estate in the area.

Still, Rob wasn't taking any chances. Whatever was up with her newest client, Hailey was not going to be alone with him any longer than Rob could help.

He packed his bag swiftly and crossed the street.

The same instinct that brought him here had him stashing his camera bag in the garage before entering the house. He could hear voices upstairs and the idea of that tanned weasel in a bedroom with Hailey had Rob's hands tightening on the handle of the cane. He didn't want it as a weapon, though he'd use the cane if he had to, he wanted it more as a prop. A kind of disguise. By leaning heavily on the thing and exaggerating his limp, he would appear feeble and unthreatening.

He made his way to the bottom of the stairs. "Hi, I'm back," he yelled.

The voices ceased. Then Hailey appeared at the top of the stairs. "Rob. What are you doing home?" her voice was friendly but he heard the steel beneath. She'd told him to make himself scarce and he was anything but.

"I have a physiotherapy appointment and my leg hurts too much to drive. I was wondering if you'd drop me off when you're finished here?"

"I—uh," she fumbled.

"If it's not out of your way?" Now he had a perfectly valid reason to stay in the house until Mr. Slick was gone.

"Okay. Just make yourself scarce until we're done."

He wasn't at all surprised to find the prospective buyer appear behind her. He'd want to check out another male in the house, especially one who was friendly enough with Hailey that she'd give him a ride.

"Hi," Rob called up the stairs, raising a friendly hand while the other white-knuckled the cane. "I'm the owner if you have any questions. Nobody knows the house like I do."

"Thanks. It's a beautiful home." The accent was East Coast. Upper-crust or faking it.

"Sure is. Too big for one person, which is why I'm selling it."

"Yes. My sister is a single mother. She and her two kids live with me. Works out for now. Of course, when I get married and start a family," he said with a glance at Hailey, "there's plenty of room here to make a suite downstairs for my sister. So we'd both have our privacy." His attitude was friendly, but his eyes were cold and Rob had the impression he was being scrutinized thoroughly. He knew the feeling since he was doing some serious scrutinizing of his own.

HAILEY WAS FURIOUS and she let Rob know it as they drove the short distance to his physio appointment. "I am not a limousine service."

"You could have said no."

"And let my client think I was heartless? No, thank you."

"Sorry." But he didn't sound very sorry. "What's his story?"

She narrowed her eyes at him. "Why?"

Rob looked at her in a way that was a little too innocent. "I'm selling a house, he wants to buy one. I wonder if he's a serious candidate. That's all."

"He's some kind of consultant in the oil business. He's spent time in the Middle East, Mexico, Texas, Alberta, all over. He wants to settle in Fremont because his extended family lives in the area."

"He have a name?"

She hesitated, but she supposed it wasn't a national secret. And her client had appeared very seriously interested in the house. "Dennis Thurgood."

Rob tapped his knee for half a block. "He seemed more interested in you than in the house," he said at last. She didn't bother telling him that she'd been at the office when the new client came in. Next thing she knew she had a new client. The front-office receptionist had giggled when she'd told Hailey that the gentleman had first asked if Hailey were a Realtor, then asked for her name, then asked if he could be her client.

The path was a little unorthodox to be sure but he was a client who was only in town for a few days with the express purpose of buying a property. He had money, knew he wanted a large home in an established neighborhood and didn't drive her crazy with nit-picky criticism. She'd felt his interest in her as a woman and was flattered by it. But she was a businesswoman first, and he was an ideal client.

Unlike the one currently at her side.

She turned to glare at him. "I think he's a serious possibility." She raised her finger, schoolmarm fashion. "Do not sabotage this deal."

"I'm not going t—"

"You've scuttled every serious possibility."

"Have not."

"What about the MacDonalds?"

"What about them?" He looked sulky and wouldn't meet her gaze.

"You told them your grandmother died in the four-poster that's the centerpiece of the master bedroom."

"They weren't the right people for the home."

"And the Fergusons?"

"Whoever heard of a little kid being terrified of raccoons?"

"And then as soon as you find that out you inform the kid that raccoons love to nest in the trees. And you had one that used to climb up to your bedroom window and you'd feed it."

"It was true."

"She made her mother take her back to the car and wouldn't come back into the house."

"I don't want anybody buying this house and not being happy here."

"It seems like everyone who's been interested hasn't been right for Bellamy House."

He scowled. "I want the right people, that's all."

She glanced over at him. He looked as though he weren't sleeping well. He barely glanced at her. She supposed it wasn't hard to figure out why.

They never should have slept together.

She'd never, ever fired a client, and with a listing as juicy as this one, she'd have a hard time doing it now, but the truth was, Rob was making her job difficult.

She sighed. "You know how you threatened to fire me?"

"I was never going to fire you." Their gazes connected and she felt a dangerous tenderness for him well up inside her.

"I think I might have to quit."

"Look," he said, "I'm having a bad day. Sorry. I shouldn't have asked you to drive me. I—I don't know how to do this. With you."

She sighed. "No. I'm sorry. Normally I'd offer to drive you to your physio. I really don't mind. It's just— I'm just—" She turned to him. Their gazes connected and everything she hadn't been able to say was right there. Between them.

She pulled up in front of the physiotherapy clinic. He didn't make a move to get out of the car.

She looked at him. He seemed to feel as lost as she did. It was all she could do not to reach over, cup his face in her hands and tell him she'd be here when he got out of his appointment. That she'd take him home to her apartment or take herself back to his place. Already her foolish heart was trying to attach to a man who didn't want commitment.

The silence stretched and then they both spoke at the same time.

"You know, I have this problem…" she began.

"I don't know what to do with my grandmother's ashes."

"I beg your pardon?" she asked.

"What?" he echoed.

It was so ridiculous she had to laugh. "You go first."

"I said, 'I don't know what to do with my grandmother's ashes.'"

She glanced at him. "Where are they now?"

"On my desk. In the house. I can't leave them there permanently obviously. I don't know where to put them."

She'd had the same problem when her father had died. Where did you put the ashes of a man who'd never belonged anywhere? In the end, she'd thrown them in the ocean at the junction of several currents in the Salish Sea. She thought that's what would have made him happiest, spreading himself all over the world.

Agnes Neeson, however, was a different person altogether.

"You know, I never knew your grandmother. Was there a place she really loved?"

He wrinkled his brow. "I can't think of any place special. That's the trouble. She was usually at the house or pottering in the backyard. That garden was a real showplace in its day.

"We used to go on holidays when I was a kid but that was for my benefit. She did most of her traveling vicariously through me."

"Rob, I think we both know where your grandmother would want her ashes to be buried. In the garden of Bellamy House."

He didn't argue. Hailey was right. It was so obvious. "She used to tell me how she and my grandfather had planned the garden, and she knew every tree. Every flower. They planted the mountain ash in the backyard because they wanted the berries to attract birds."

"Don't you think that's the perfect spot for her final resting place?"

"But people think the mountain ash is a garbage tree. They might chop it down. Pave over the whole backyard and churn my grandmother into tarmac. Then how would I feel? The new owners might pull down the old place and put up some big new McMansion."

"All you can do is your best, Rob."

"I guess. I'll think about it." He turned to her. "What were you going to say? Something about a problem?"

"I— Oh, I feel stupid now."

"More stupid than me asking what to do with a dead woman's ashes?"

"Right. Okay. Well, here's the thing. I have this problem. I think I've had it for a long time. Because we moved around so much, I became really good at fitting in." She fiddled with the key ring hanging from her ignition. It was a diamond slipper, given to her by Julia for her last birthday. "That's why I'm good at sales. I learned how to connect with strangers really fast. It's how I survived."

He nodded.

"The secret of being able to move when you've barely settled and start one more time in one more new school in one more new town is not to attach too securely." She glanced at him, "Does this make sense?"

He nodded.

"I made friends with so many girls along the way. Girls I didn't keep in contact with. Girls I probably wouldn't recognize if they walked past me on the street. I left one place and had to put all my energies in surviving in the next town. I couldn't waste energy on the past."

"Sure. Makes sense. You know, your voice, it goes higher when you talk about this stuff."

She touched her throat. Went "ahem" a couple of times to clear the constriction.

"It's hard for you to talk about. That's why your voice rises."

She nodded. Surprised he'd know something she'd needed a therapist to explain. As an interviewer he'd be acute to things like voice and tone. He could probably tell her that her shoulders were up a little higher than normal, too. She forced herself to relax.

"Why is that a problem? You seem fine now. You and Julia are obviously close."

She smiled. "Julia's the best friend I've ever had. Yet she had to work with me to get me there. She was the one who suggested counseling." Then she fell serious again. "That's not the problem. The issue I have is that somehow in my strange upbringing—or maybe I'm just hardwired this way—I can't do that with men."

He seemed confused. "What do you mean, exactly?"

"I attach. Weirdly and way too fast." She touched her chest. "I have to be so careful with my heart."

He felt a funny sensation in his own chest, a cross between a pain and an itch. He'd never had such a feeling in his life.

He also felt as though his collar was too tight. And

he wasn't wearing a collar. That feeling he'd had plenty. He edged closer to the door. "Are you saying…"

She shook her head, a wry smile on her face. "That I'm in love with you? No. What I'm saying is that I have to be very careful or I will be." She sighed. "And that can't end well for me."

He opened his mouth. Closed it again. Pondered. "Is that why you have that crazy-ass notion that you have to get your career going now and settle down later?"

"Mostly I just say that to protect myself. The truth is, if a local man was interested in me and he was a settling-down kind of guy, then I'd be interested."

"Like that guy looking at my house?"

She licked her lips. "Theoretically."

"He's asked you out, hasn't he?"

Damn, he was good. Those shrewd blue eyes didn't miss much. "Yep."

"Hunh. You're right. That is a problem."

15

ROB WENT THROUGH the photos he'd snapped of Dennis Thurgood, aka Mr. Slick, then uploaded several choice images to his computer.

The man had done nothing more sinister than act edgy around a cop car.

And ask Hailey out.

Maybe he'd have let it go except the man was coming back for another look at the house, which meant he'd be spending more time alone with Hailey. When she'd let slip that he wouldn't be needing a mortgage, Rob's suspicions had intensified.

Rob had no proof of anything. Yet…something about the guy was off.

Okay, he might be making a fool of himself. If his grandmother could speak to him from inside that box, he knew what she'd say. "Wouldn't be the first time."

He called his editor in New York.

It wasn't jealousy, he told himself, as he studied the images again. Listening to his gut instincts had saved lives, and not only his own.

Gary took the call right away. "Rob, good to hear from you. How's the leg?"

"Not bad. Healing."

"You running six-minute miles yet?"

"Funny. I'm in physiotherapy. She says she'll have me running in a week. Two tops."

"That's great. I could use you in the field."

"Yeah. I know. I follow the news."

Gary was one of the busiest people Rob knew so he didn't waste any more time in idle conversation. "Gary, I need a favor."

"What is it?" His tone sharpened. Rob could picture his boss pulling a notepad toward him, clicking open his ballpoint.

"I want you to run a check on someone."

"You're on sick leave. What the hell are you doing?" he said, sounding frustrated.

"I swear I didn't do anything. And I could be completely mistaken, but there's this guy who wants to buy my grandmother's house. I think something's shady about him."

He described the incident with the cop car.

Gary didn't sound impressed. "He could have unpaid parking tickets. Come on. You're not used to living in suburbia. You're bored. You're seeing things."

"I hope you're right. I really do. Could you do this for me? As a friend? For the guy who'd take a bullet to get you the hottest news."

"That is a low blow, even for you. What do you care who buys your house? So long as he's got the cash?"

There was a pause. Rob might bend the truth a little now and then, but he never lied to Gary. "There's a woman involved."

"Ah."

"I can't explain it. I think she could be in danger from this guy."

A long-suffering sigh traveled the miles between them. "What have you got?"

"Photos. And a name and occupation that may or may not be false."

"Send me what you've got. I'll see what I can do."

"Thanks."

"I'm making no promises. I'll see what I can do."

"Got it."

He emailed the photos and as much information about Mr. Slick as he'd been able to pry out of Hailey. It wasn't much but Gary had connections like nobody else. He never revealed how he got the information he did, and Rob never asked. All he could do was hope Gary would take him seriously.

And that—for once—his famous instincts were wrong.

He needed activity. He could go to the gym and do the workout his physiotherapist had created for him but he needed to be outdoors. The day was warm for September, short-sleeves-and-sunglasses nice.

He looked at his grandmother's remains and made a second call.

"Hi, Rob," Hailey said when she answered.

"Thanks for taking my call. I want to ask you something."

"What is it?"

"Would you come over and help me bury my grandmother? I feel like it should be special somehow. You're the only person I want to be there."

There was a silence and he felt all the things they couldn't say. How he wished he could be different for her. How she wished the same.

"Of course I'll come. I'm honored to be asked."

"Thank you."

She showed up an hour later with a bag from a local garden store. In it were spring bulbs and a small metal plaque with the gardener's prayer engraved on it.

He felt a rush of emotion fill him. "It's from a poem by Dorothy Gurney. My grandmother loved it." He felt such a connection between these two women. He'd made the right choice in asking Hailey to be part of this small ceremony to mark his grandmother's burial.

He dug the hole with a dirt-encrusted shovel he found in the shed. Neither of them said anything as he emptied the box of ashes into the hole. He wasn't a praying man but he felt an enormous sense of rightness in putting her ashes under the shade of the mountain ash.

Hailey helped him plant the tulip and daffodil bulbs. Then he covered over the hole and pushed the stake holding the plaque into the freshly dug earth.

He read aloud, hoping that somewhere his grandmother could hear him:

The kiss of the sun for pardon,
The song of the birds for mirth,
One is nearer God's heart in a garden
Than anywhere else on earth.

WHEN THE SIMPLE BURIAL was done, he turned to Hailey. She was wearing a flowered dress and he suspected she'd changed in order to wear the perfect outfit to say goodbye to a woman she'd never even met.

Rob had never felt more bereft.

"Don't go," he said.

She shook her head. Her eyes were luminous and he felt that she belonged here as surely as his grandmother did.

He walked to her, took her in his arms. She didn't resist.

Without a word, they walked into the house through the back door and, hand in hand, made their way upstairs.

This time he didn't hesitate. He took Hailey to the room he now thought of as his.

The big four-poster looked as solid as his grandparents' marriage had been. And Hailey's hand in his felt as solid, as true and lasting.

He wasn't sure he had it in him to give her what she wanted. What she deserved. Still he turned her to him, kissed her slowly and softly said, "I can't promise—"

He didn't finish. She laid a finger across his lips. "I know," she said. "It's okay."

He kissed that finger. Slid his own fingers along her palm and opened them so he could kiss her open palm, then her wrist where a pulse beat rapidly against his lips. The heat coming off her skin, the scent that was hers alone, intoxicated him.

As he undid the buttons at the front of her dress, he kissed the top of each breast following the lacy edge of her bra with his lips, making her sigh with quiet pleasure. When he had all the buttons undone, he eased the dress off her shoulders and it slid to the floor, resembling a pool of flowers.

Kneeling before her, he kissed down her belly, down to panties that were as lacy and erotic as that bra. When he slipped his thumbs into the sides and slid them down her legs she shivered. He could feel a trembling in her limbs, felt her arousal, mirroring his. He was so hard he felt he might explode. Knowing they'd end up making love on the floor if he continued doing what he wanted to, he rose, unhooked her bra, let himself enjoy the sight of her bare breasts, then pulled back the covers on the big bed and laid her down. It seemed to him as though the bed welcomed them with open arms.

"I want you naked," she informed him in a sultry tone.

She watched as he stripped for her, which he did in record time, and then he knelt between her legs and loved her with his mouth. Her hands tangled in his hair as he took her up, feeling her excitement build, tasting it on his tongue.

When she reached her first peak, she cried out, bucking against him, and then to his delight, she yanked on his hair. "I need you inside me," she moaned.

He managed to hold on to enough sanity to mumble, "Condom," and race to the bathroom. He brought out a handful and sheathed himself with fumbling hands. He'd never wanted anything as much as he wanted to be inside this woman.

He looked into her eyes, and, as his body entered hers, he let her see all the emotions he couldn't find another way to express.

As their passion built, she reached behind her, clasping one of the bedposts, as though it could keep her tethered to earth. He raised his hand, found hers and clasped it and the mahogany post as they rocketed to heaven together.

16

"I DON'T EVEN WANT to go home," John said. He and Julia were trying a new Thai place that had received good reviews. It was the second time this week they'd grabbed dinner. "My wife did all the decorating. I'm living in a box with beige walls and the furniture my ex didn't want."

"How bad is it?" Julia had to ask.

"Pretty bad."

He'd been good to her. So the online dating thing hadn't turned up much in the way of dates; she'd found a friend. And it was nice to have a man to go to a movie with and hang out with.

"I'd be happy to come over and give you some ideas."

"Really? Because I was totally hinting."

She chuckled. "I got that."

"Would tomorrow afternoon work? You could give me some ideas and then we could go for dinner somewhere."

"No hot dates?" she teased.

"Not hardly. You?"

"I'll be at your place at two o'clock."

"Great."

When she arrived at his house a little after two-thirty, she quickly realized he hadn't exaggerated. The place he'd bought was a standard bungalow with every interior wall painted the same shade of beige.

The place had definite possibilities though.

The rooms were a good size, the original oak floors had been refinished and large picture windows let in a ton of light.

The furniture, however, was pitiful. The kind of bad rec-room stuff you banish to the basement until you have the money to upgrade. Seemed like he and his wife had never got around to upgrading.

His bedroom furniture consisted of a queen-size mattress on the floor.

After ten minutes of walking through the house, she said, "I need a budget.'

"Already?"

"Yup. I need to know what you're prepared to spend." She took out her computer tablet. "There are emergency items, essentials and nice to have. We'll prioritize."

"Let me put it to you this way. If I let you do everything you want, how much would it cost?"

She smiled. "That's the sort of budget I like."

When he opened his mouth to protest—probably—she said, "Okay, okay. Here's where I want to start. First, the reason I was a teeny bit late is that I had some paint leftover from another job. And it's ideal for here. We'll do the main downstairs rooms in a color called linen. Don't worry, it's very neutral. Masculine in fact. You'll love it. I also snagged some mascarpone. That's for woodwork and trim. If you feel like a handyman project, you can do those horrible kitchen cupboards yourself. Otherwise, we send them out." She patted his shoulder. "So the paint's free."

"Why do I get the feeling that nothing else is?"

She tapped on the computer tablet in her hand. "I get a discount on furniture at several terrific places. Honestly, John, you need to get rid of this crap. Now."

He leaned against a beige wall and folded his arms. He had nice, muscular arms, she noticed. "That sounds like shopping. I hate shopping."

"You could give me your credit card and stay home."

"I can do shopping."

"Let's go then."

He looked alarmed. "What? Now?"

"There's no better time. And trust me. When you have a home that suits you and feels comfortable, you're going to enjoy being here."

"You're the professional. Let's go."

You LEARNED A LOT ABOUT a person when you attempted to remake their home as Julia knew from experience. In John's case he was easy to deal with, accepting all her suggestions and only quibbling when she tried to get him to move his big-screen TV out of the living room.

"Absolutely not," he said. "I watch games in here. I'm the one that does the living in the living room. What's the point of sticking me in a spare bedroom? The fireplace is out here. It's close to the kitchen. The big screen stays."

"Fine," she said. It was his house, after all, and his argument made sense. Once they'd chosen the furniture—well, she'd chosen, and he'd pulled out his credit card—they were ready for a break. As they headed for a local Mexican restaurant that she loved, they walked past a trendy menswear shop. She glanced in the window, then at her companion who wore his usual collection of unfortunate clothing choices.

Should she?

She glanced at him walking beside her. He had a great body, but he always camouflaged it in a series of clothing disasters. He'd been good about letting her re-decorate his home. Maybe?

"John," she said, her tone tentative.

"I don't like that look in your eye. I'm not buying three identical white vases to place on the mantel."

"No. It's not about vases. Honestly. I was just wondering whether you'd like to check out this menswear shop."

He narrowed his eyes at her. "Why would I want to do that?"

She shrugged. "No reason. I think those jeans would look really good on you."

He wasn't fooled. "Are you trying to stage me, too?"

She nibbled her lower lip. Truth or not? She decided, since they were friends and not lovers, that she could afford honesty.

"I don't mean to be rude, but you could look so much better. You've got good bone structure, a nice body, but your clothes aren't doing you any favors."

"I like to be comfortable."

"And that was fine when you were married. Now that you're single, I think you should work on present-ing your best package."

He snorted with laughter. Realizing what she'd said, she blushed. "I don't mean that package... Oh, you know."

He stared in the window. "If I put those jeans on, they'll definitely be all about my package. Those things are tight."

"At least try them on."

She coaxed him into the store and soon she had him

in a fitting room with a selection of jeans, sweaters and shirts.

He emerged wearing jeans that actually fit. She couldn't believe the difference. He had a seriously nice body. And, she couldn't help but notice there did seem to be a pretty nice package in there.

She pushed him in front of the full-length mirror. "See how much better these look?"

"They'd better. They cost almost as much as that sectional sofa you talked me into."

Still, he had a half smile on his face.

In half an hour she'd talked him into a pair of jeans, black pants for going out, a casual shirt, a sweater and leather shoes that could be casual or dressed up. As a wardrobe went it was pretty basic. However, like her decorating project, you started with the emergency list. There were plenty more items she could add to bolster his wardrobe. At least he had a start.

"And there's a really good stylist near my office called Savoir Faire. Felix is the owner's name. He does terrific men's cuts. I could—"

He held up a hand. "Enough. I can only take so much improvement in one day."

"So HE HELD UP HIS HAND and said—" and here Julia lowered her voice in a truly bad imitation of a man "'—Enough. I can only take so much improvement in one day.'"

Hailey laughed dutifully. Well, it was funny, but she was having trouble concentrating. She really needed to pull herself together. She and Julia were shopping. Hailey for something to wear on her date with Dennis, who'd checked out the hottest new eateries before inviting her. She liked that he'd taken the initiative, and not used the fact that she was the local and he an out-of-towner as an excuse to make her choose the restaurant.

She'd heard nothing but rave reviews about Gastronome, raves on everything but the prices, which were steep.

Julia was shopping mostly because she loved shopping.

"John sounds like a nice guy," Hailey said to Julia, who was currently flipping through a rack of red and black tops as though she didn't already own enough black and red.

"Oh, he is." Julia glanced up. "And I think there's a surprisingly nice-looking man hiding under all that crap."

"Not for you?"

Her friend shrugged. "I'm regifting him to some deserving woman." Then she found a short black cocktail dress. "Ooh, I bet Dennis would love you in this."

Hailey would not feel guilty. She would not feel bad that she had accepted a date with her latest client. Why shouldn't she date?

It wasn't as if Rob had anything to offer her. Except the greatest sex of her life and an intimacy between them that was about so much more than sex.

If only he were a stay-at-home man.

Or she were a different kind of woman.

If there was one thing Rob had done for her, it was get her thinking about schedules and life plans and how perhaps hers was too rigid. It wasn't as though she could plan that in five years, when her business was more successful and she felt settled and ready, her ideal man would suddenly appear. Instead, she was beginning to realize that a little flexibility was a good thing, whether in life, in business or in love.

She was bending her own strict rules and dating a client. So what?

She found herself staring at a dress she didn't even like. "I don't know. I feel like I want to stay away from black."

"Right." Julia went to put it back on the rack, then said, "Maybe I'll try it on. I wonder if they have my size."

As Hailey flipped through dress after dress, she tried to imagine dating Dennis.

He was intelligent; he was charming; he loved Bellamy House almost as much as she did. What was it to Rob who bought the place? He clearly didn't want to keep his grandmother's house.

She tried not to contemplate what it would be like to date a guy who owned Bellamy House. One who wasn't Rob. She couldn't picture being with anyone else in that wonderful home. Somehow, in her mind, it would always be his.

Well, as Gloria had reminded her, she needed to stop wasting the present by worrying about the future. Everything would work out, she was certain of it.

Dennis had been suddenly called out of town for a few days but had made her promise she'd call him if any other serious buyers for Bellamy House appeared. She'd agreed. And had also agreed to postpone their date. Since she and Julia had already decided to go shopping, however, they'd kept that date.

She felt so torn. So messed up. And suddenly she realized that that was why women have each other. To talk to.

"Hey, how about we ditch the shopping and grab lunch early? I need to talk."

"Of course," her friend said, instantly putting the dress back.

Maybe a few days was exactly what she needed to get some perspective. Sleeping with Rob a second time had been the mistake she'd known it would be.

Well, she kind of thought her big mistake was sleeping with him in the first place. Her plan hadn't worked, not at all. Think about him less once she got him into bed?

She snorted at her own foolishness.

Over lunch at a little bistro around the corner she told Julia all of it.

Her friend opened her eyes wide. "You had sex on that single bed?"

"Yes."

"And that was the best sex of your life? On a single bed?"

She nodded.

"With a man with a bullet hole in his leg?"

"Uh-huh."

Julia stared at her as she sipped her tea. "Can you imagine what he'd be like in a real bed? With all his limbs working properly?"

They both sighed.

"Well, our second time was in the four-poster."

The teacup hit its saucer with a snap. "Second time? I thought you said—"

"I did. But we'd buried his grandmother's ashes, and he was so sad and so sweet, and he looked at me and I was lost."

"I know. Burying people always makes me hot."

She laughed. They both did. This was why it was so great to have a friend. For all her sarcasm Julia got it.

Their laughter died and she said, "In that big bed. I

can't explain it. The sex was so different. It was slower, the connection was so deep, it was like, like…"

"Like you were in love with him?"

Her friend's warm brown eyes were full of sympathy.

Hailey smacked her forehead into her palm. "I've gone and fallen in love with Rob. When I promised myself I wouldn't. It was only going to be one night. Just one night…"

"And now you're in love with him."

"Yeah."

"What about him? Is he in love with you?"

She thought about how he'd looked at her after they'd planted the tulips, how tenderly he'd made love to her. "Yes. I think he is. That doesn't change anything though. He's still the man with the camera on the other side of the world. And I'm still the girl who wants a stay-at-home guy."

"What are you going to do?"

As much as she didn't want to, Hailey knew she had to move on. "I'm going to date Dennis. And maybe a few other men I find interesting. And Rob will heal and he'll return to his globe-trotting existence. And I will try to forget him."

Her friend's response was succinct. "That plan sucks."

"Can you think of a better one?"

"Nope."

17

JULIA WAS IN A HURRY to see John's house completed, though not as much of a hurry as he was in, which made the project fun to work on.

She called in the painters she always used. They were fast and reliable, and more important, could come immediately. She'd chosen a chocolate color for his bedroom. During the week she'd spent extra time picking linens and a few accessories that she knew he wouldn't have been interested in.

The furniture was being delivered on Saturday and she was as excited as if it were her own home she was decorating.

When he called her Friday she assumed it was to let her know what time all the furniture was going to be delivered the next day.

It wasn't. "How do you feel about dinner?" he asked.

"Enthusiastic. I'm a big believer in three squares a day."

"Very funny. How do you feel about dinner tonight? With me?"

"Even more enthusiastic. I absolutely do not feel like cooking tonight."

"Seven?"

"Perfect."

"Pick you up?"

She hesitated. "Hmm. Tempting. I'm staging a place downtown. I don't think I'm going to have time to go home first. Why don't I meet you someplace?"

"Indian sound good to you?"

"Yes."

"You're a very easy woman to please."

She chuckled. "You're hitting all the right notes."

He named a place she'd heard of but never tried, and they agreed to meet at seven.

The staging job took longer than she'd anticipated. After she'd plumped the last cushion and fussed with the final flower arrangement she saw she was running a few minutes late. However, she absolutely could not be seen in public without retouching her makeup, which she did in the car once she'd parked near the restaurant.

When she walked in, she couldn't see John at first. There were two men sitting alone at tables, but a quick scan showed neither was him. Both were well-turned out, obviously waiting for their wives or dates. She glanced at her watch. Okay, she was a quarter of an hour late, but surely he wouldn't…

She started to nibble on her freshly lipsticked lip when one of the two men waved at her.

"John?" She couldn't have been more shocked. He stood and came toward her. "You look so different." She'd seen potential there, but even she hadn't seen how hot he could be. "What have you done?"

He was wearing the jeans she'd talked him into and the black sweater, which reminded her how good his body was.

But there was so much more he'd done to himself.

They returned to his table and he said, "I took your advice. I went to Savoir Faire and had my hair styled." He put air quotes around *styled* but he'd gone, hadn't he?

"I can't believe the difference a good cut makes."

"The guy who did the cutting is the one who recommended the eyeglass place."

"That's what else is different. Your glasses are from this millennium. They look good. You have beautiful eyes."

He seemed slightly embarrassed by her enthusiasm for his new look and quickly changed the subject.

"How did your staging go today?"

"Fine. The Realtor was really pleased. He's going to put photos on his website and mention First Impressions by name. It's always good to get a little free publicity."

While they talked, a woman walked by and Julia could see her checking John out. She wasn't used to seeing him ogled and she was surprised at how much she didn't like the experience.

"Have you had any dates since your makeover?" she asked him.

"A couple." Again that unusual stab of irritation. Why shouldn't he date?

"And?"

What was she doing, she wondered, offering her time and talents to turn John into a great-looking guy with a stylish home just so she could gift him to another woman?

He sat back, sipped the ginger drink they'd both ordered, and said, "The first one was nice enough. She was early for our date."

Julia thought of her own perpetual tardiness and hated this woman on principle. "She probably has no life," she commented.

"Could be. But then, if being early means you have no life, I guess I don't have one either."

"Oops."

"You know what's weird?"

"What?"

"I've got used to having that time to myself while I wait for you. I find it kind of relaxing. Have a drink, check email on my cell, settle in and study the menu. I didn't like this woman arriving at the same time as me. It threw me."

This was good. She was starting to feel better. "What about the other date?"

He shook his head. "I suggested coffee, but she wanted to go for a drink instead. Talked nonstop about herself while getting plastered. I put her in a cab two hours after we met. Longest two hours of my life."

"I'm only a social drinker," Julia said. Which was a stupid thing to say and completely irrelevant to the conversation. Especially as they'd already decided they were only going to be friends.

"I've noticed."

She looked up. Their gazes caught and held for a moment. She felt as though she were seeing him for the first time. He was already familiar to her, and yet, tonight he seemed different. Sexier. Surer of himself, maybe.

She glanced down again and the strange moment passed.

As dinner progressed the evening seemed more like a date. She found herself feeling flirty and felt a similar vibe coming from her companion.

A pleasant sense of uncertainty teased at her. They'd agreed they didn't have chemistry. Was it possible they'd been wrong?

Was it simply that they hadn't given each other a chance? She studied him across the table and saw not a fashion model nor a Greek god, but a real flesh-and-blood man. A heck of a lot better put together than the one she'd first met, but he wasn't a fantasy. She already knew that he was a stickler about time—though he seemed able to cope with her habit of being slightly late. She knew from his house that he was absurdly tidy—again, not something they had in common. She kept her place clean, but was always fighting clutter.

He enjoyed trying new restaurants. As did she. They could talk about anything and everything from places they'd traveled to bands they both liked or didn't to local politics.

He'd become a good friend. Could he be more?

Once outside the restaurant, they lingered a moment too long. She didn't want to leave him. He didn't seem in a hurry to leave her.

"It's a funny thing about dating sites," he said. "You end up judging people so fast. It's like you have these ideas about what you want and like and if the other person doesn't hit a bunch of the things in the first few minutes of meeting, you move on."

"Sometimes too fast, maybe."

"Yes. Exactly." He stepped closer to her. "I have to make a confession."

Her pulse sped up. "What is it?" She hoped it wasn't something bad. She *really* hoped it wasn't something bad.

He said, "I was attracted to you the first time we met."

"You were?"

"Yep. You obviously weren't into me so I figured friends was still good."

"I was caught up in my ridiculous fantasy." She closed her eyes. "I was so naive."

"Do you still just want to be friends? Or are you open to something more?"

In response, she stepped even closer to him until she could see the black flecks in his blue eyes that were staring into hers with an intensity that she felt throughout her being. She raised herself on tiptoe. She'd intended to kiss him. Somewhere along the line, though, he took over, drawing her in tight and kissing her long and hard. It was a kiss that could make a woman forget to breathe.

When he pulled away, she touched his face. "Oh, I am definitely willing to consider more."

"Good."

She fiddled with her car keys. "I've got some linens I picked up for you in the car."

"The bedroom furniture arrived today. Do you want to come and see it?"

His gaze was tender, and she didn't feel like speaking, maybe wasn't able to. She just nodded.

He nodded back. Sometimes you didn't need words.

She climbed into her car and followed him back to his place. She felt jumpy and strange, but also keenly excited. She was pretty sure they were going to do more with that bed than put linens on it. Luckily, her gym bag was in the car so she had toiletries, a few cosmetics, a toothbrush and a change of underwear—an unexpected benefit of belonging to the gym.

When she walked into his house she cried out in delight. Against the freshly painted walls rested the new furniture. Clearly the bedroom suite wasn't the only furniture that had been delivered a day early.

"The sectional is great there. And wasn't I right about

the paint color and those black-and-white photographs? Masculine but stylish. Even the TV fits in now."

Even though this was her business there was huge pride when her design worked out. As this one had.

"What do you think?" she asked him.

"Beautiful," he said, not looking at the freshly painted walls or the brand-new furniture. He was looking at her.

She held the bag of linens in one hand, her gym bag and purse over the other shoulder. He walked over, took the bag from her hands. "Would you like to see the bedroom?"

"Very much."

When they entered his bedroom, she barely noticed the decor. All she saw was that splendid Mission-style bed. Already made.

"It looks fantastic," she said.

"I haven't slept in it yet."

To be the first in his bed was a wonderful thing, she decided. "New beginnings are good."

He took her into his arms, kissed her slowly, and then he knelt and scooped her up.

"What are you doing? I weigh a ton."

"No, you don't." And he laid her down on his bed.

He left the bedside lamps on, and for once, she didn't insist on darkness. If he was brave enough to lift her, she figured he knew she had a pound or ten she'd love to get rid of. He hadn't groaned or toppled under her weight. He didn't even seem to be breathing hard. She supposed he could handle her.

He took his time undressing her. When her full breasts spilled out as he took off her bra, he made a sound of pleasure and reached down to pop a plump nipple in his mouth. She felt lazy, content to be toyed with, as he learned her body, explored her hills and valleys, coaxing her slowly until she didn't feel lazy anymore. He slipped a hand between her thighs, drove her up higher until she crested the first peak crying out against his mouth.

"You're dressed," she said, when she could focus once more.

"Not for long."

She watched him, taking as much pleasure in eyeing his body as he had in revealing hers.

"You don't care at all that I have a few extra pounds on me, do you?"

"I like you exactly the way you are."

She sighed with deep contentment. Then she reached for him. "Let me show you what a woman with a few extra pounds can do with them."

18

ROB DECIDED TO BE COOL. So Hailey had a date with a smarmy twit who didn't like cops? It wasn't like she would go back to his hotel room or something on the first date.

He upped the weight on the leg press and powered through a few more reps. He didn't even think about the pain, only about getting strong again. Getting his mobility back.

Rob needed his quad muscles to be completely functional. Not only did he need to run a mile in six, he needed to be strong enough to run away from Fremont, from his memories, from Bellamy House, and most of all, from Hailey.

It bothered him even to admit how that woman had burrowed under his skin. No, when he thought about it, she hadn't burrowed at all. She'd blasted into his system with the same impact as that bullet. And there were moments when he thought the damage she'd done wouldn't heal as fast. Or be as relatively painless.

"You using that bench?" a gym-jock grunted at him, indicating the bench where he'd rested his towel.

He shook his head. Kept pushing. Five more reps.

He'd do five more reps then he'd take a break. As beads of sweat slid down his temple, he hunched a shoulder and wiped it onto his T-shirt. Three more. He could do it. He'd push through the pain.

The sooner he was out of here the better. He'd head back for New York. Pick up the pieces of his normal nomadic life. He tried to picture a reunion with Romona, but the fantasy wouldn't come. He could only think about Hailey. How he'd started out enjoying the challenge, the teasing to get the woman into his bed and the utter mind-blowing passion they'd experienced together once he had.

She'd warned him that she was afraid to fall in love and he'd tried to respect that, backing off out of courtesy to her.

Okay, they'd fallen into bed one more time but neither had planned that. He couldn't stop thinking about those hours in that four-poster and how everything had felt so utterly right. A final puzzle piece had fitted into place. Click.

One more rep. Every muscle in his body was bunched as he pushed up against the weight. It felt as if he were lifting a million pounds with his ankle while someone was stabbing this thigh with a hot poker.

The irony was they'd both worried about her heart. Who'd given a rat's ass about his?

Nobody, that's who. And now look at him. Trying to build up enough strength to run.

Because the truth was it wasn't Hailey who was in trouble here. It was him.

Mr. Lighthearted, the traveling guy who never stayed in one place long enough to get caught. And here he was, as caught as any man could be.

He was so in love with that woman he ached with it. But that didn't change who he was.

He hobbled off the machine, grabbed his towel and dried his wet face.

And that didn't change who she was.

Nobody knew better than he did that love wasn't enough.

He showered and returned home, driving Gran's Buick down streets as familiar as his own memories. He was pulling into the drive when his cell phone shrilled.

"I ran a mile in eight minutes yesterday," he said.

"Hello to you, too."

"Merv?" He checked his cell again. "What's my agent doing calling from my editor's office?"

"We were talking about you."

"I know he wants me back. I'm ready. Really."

"Rob, I'm not the HR department. Gary and I were talking about your photojournal."

"Photojournal?"

"That's what we're calling it. *My Neighborhood.* A photojournal. We're both excited about the possibilities. You've captured how people have parallel interests and concern wherever they live, whatever their relative wealth or political situation. It works because you always come back to your own hometown. Fremont becomes the central character in the book. And the photos are some of your best work."

"Oh, right. The book idea." He'd almost forgotten he'd sent Merv the photos and idea.

"More than a book idea. Gary and I talked about doing something interesting. *World Week*'s parent company, Anvil Media, also has a book publishing arm, as you know."

"Sure."

"Gary and I are discussing a book that also has a magazine and website component."

He shut the engine off. Got out. Wandered toward the mountain ash tree. "Not sure I follow."

He wanted his grandmother to hear this. He settled himself on the cool ground, his back leaning against the tree trunk, his throbbing leg stretched out before him.

"It's simple. Anvil publishes the coffee-table book, you agree to do a number of features for the magazine based on the same idea. Cross publicity for the book and the magazine. Maybe a few extra pieces exclusive to the web."

"I don't do features. I cover hard news."

"Until a few weeks ago, you didn't write coffee-table books either."

"What kind of money are we talking?"

Merv told him. His eyebrows rose. He repeated the sum for his grandmother's benefit. "That's a nice chunk of change."

"You bet. Think about it. Gary says you'll still be a hard-news guy but this gives you a little more breathing room. Might stop you from burning out."

Or getting bored. He nearly jumped out of his skin. He could have sworn his grandmother's voice had uttered those words.

And, as so often, he thought she might be right.

He wondered how much of his travel bug had been simple boredom? The truth was, since he'd been home this time he hadn't felt bored once. With Hailey trying to sell the house to hordes of the wrong types and *My Neighborhood* to keep him busy and wanting to get Hailey into bed, enjoying the greatest sex of his life when he did, then wishing he could get her back into his bed, he hadn't had much time to be idle.

He patted the ground where tulips would bloom come spring and he wouldn't be here to see them.

Unless.

He realized he needed to tell Hailey his good news. He called her.

"Hi, Rob."

"Hi. I want to talk to you about something." He didn't want to tell her his news over the phone. He wanted to watch her face, to share his excitement. "How would it be if I take you for dinner?"

"When?"

"Tonight."

There was a tiny pause. "I can't tonight. I already have a date."

His good mood dimmed as though a light had been switched off. "A date."

"Yes."

"Would this date be with Dennis Thurgood?"

"Yes."

"I don't think you should go. I don't trust that guy."

"You met him for five minutes. You don't know a thing about him."

"I saw him. When you were showing him the house. He turned his head when a cop car went by."

This time the pause was longer. "Were you spying on us?"

"No. Not exactly. I happened to be across the street at the park."

"With a telescope?"

"A telephoto lens. It was purely coincidence."

"And through studying a man through a camera lens for a couple of minutes you've decided...what exactly?"

"I don't know," he admitted. "How he turned his

head as the cruiser went by looked suspicious. An innocent man doesn't care if a cop gets a good look at him."

"That's it? That's your entire reason for telling me not to go out with a man? There might be a million reasons why he turned his head. Maybe he thought he was going to sneeze. Or he was checking out the state of the siding. He is interested in buying the house, you know."

"I have a bad feeling."

"You're paranoid."

He traced the words of that poem on the plaque she'd bought. "I was right about your friend and the Nigerian scammer."

"Even she figured that one out."

"Don't go."

"Give me a better reason why I shouldn't go."

"I want to talk to you. I—I…" What was the use?

She sighed. "I need to get going. I'll talk to you tomorrow."

"Where's he taking you? On this date?"

"So you can turn up with your telephoto lens? I don't think so," she said, ending the call.

ROB SHOWERED, CHANGED INTO a clean pair of jeans and a gray sweater and decided that if it was date night here in Seattle he didn't feel like spending it sitting around in the house feeling sorry for himself with nothing better to do than imagine Hailey out with Mr. Slick.

He didn't feel like hooking up with one of his old friends.

There was a neighborhood watering hole not far from here where he could sit at the bar, enjoy a beer, get something to eat and watch the Mariners.

He looked at the keys to the Buick and decided that

one beer might too easily stretch into three. He'd leave the car and grab a cab.

Rain was falling when he stepped out. Ridiculous city. Always dripping. Who'd want to live in a rainforest? Not him.

He gave directions and the driver said, "Going to the bar to watch the game, huh?"

"Absolutely."

And he was treated to the cabbie's views on the Mariners. He experienced a strange sense of disconnection. He could so easily be one of those guys who followed teams and put money on fantasy leagues and whatever men who lived in one place for extended periods of time did.

He'd never missed that sort of life because he'd never envisioned it. Still, as the cab splashed its way through the wet streets, he began to warm up to the idea.

Hell, it was a cold, wet night and the idea of some male bonding over a game sounded good.

He paid the driver and entered the noisy place. There was one seat left at the bar. Empty because it was closest to the big screen and he'd have to crane his neck to see. Since his other choice was standing and his leg hurt like a son of a bitch, he took the barstool.

After ordering a beer, he started to watch the game. Groans, shouts of encouragement, cheers punctuated the play. They were the people of his neighborhood, he supposed, if he'd ever really had a neighborhood. They were professionals with ties bunched in their pockets, stopping to watch some baseball on their way home from work. They were soccer moms and dads. The plumbers and electricians he'd call if something needed fixing. They were groups of guys who liked to hang out together and a few singles like him who didn't want to sit home alone.

Especially not when the woman he'd fallen in love with was out on the town with another guy.

He took a pull of his beer, cold and smooth going down his throat. He rubbed the back of his neck, wishing the prickling sensation would go away. Hailey was fine. Maybe she had terrible taste in dates but she wasn't in a jungle surrounded by rebel forces wanting to harm her. She was an intelligent woman in a big city.

She'd be fine.

He tried to concentrate on the game but he couldn't stop thinking about her. About everything she was communicating to him by dating another man.

And what had he communicated to her? By stepping out of the way and letting her go?

Maybe that's what his irritation was about. It wasn't her in danger, it was him. In danger of losing the most amazing woman he'd ever met.

"What a fool!" he suddenly blurted aloud.

"I know, man," the chunky guy beside him said. "He totally shoulda seen that comin."

They both had their eyes on the screen. "Yeah," Rob agreed. "He should have seen it coming."

Tomorrow, he'd call her.

And what?

Was he really thinking about changing his life dramatically? For a woman?

His pocket buzzed and he realized it was his cell, which he'd put on vibrate. He glanced at the call display. "Gary? Why you calling so late?" He calculated it must be after eleven in New York.

"Where are you?"

"What? Oh, in a bar."

"Go somewhere quiet. Now."

19

GARY WASN'T A MAN to give orders without serious reason. Every nerve in Rob's body went into heightened alert. He rose from the bar, tossed money on the counter and walked out to the relative quiet of the street.

"I'm outside. What is it?"

"Those pics you sent me? Of the guy you wanted checked out?"

His fight-or-flight response was on full alert. Only there was no flight. It was all fight. "What about him?"

"Is he still in Seattle?"

"He left for a while but he's back. Why?"

"Your instincts are the best I've ever seen. Dennis Thurgood is a person of extreme interest to Interpol, the CIA and the DEA."

"Holy shit. What'd he do?"

"He's a real bad dude. Drugs and arms mostly. He almost got caught in a big bust in Paris a few months ago. Nobody knew he'd snuck into the States. The best guess is he's trying to hide out."

Rob thought of the fact the man had said he wouldn't need a mortgage. "You can add money-laundering to the list."

"Any idea where Thurgood is now?"

He wanted to punch something. "Out with my girl."

"Where?"

"I don't know." Fear, anxiety, anger churned in his gut and he had to tamp them down or he was no good to anybody. He forced himself to calm down. Think.

"They were going for dinner. I'll find out where."

"You call me when you find out where they are and I'll relay the information to the right people."

"Yeah."

"Do *not* be the hero. Let the pros handle it."

He didn't waste time arguing. There was no time. He ended the call.

Hit the button that would connect him with Hailey. "Come on," he urged. "Pick up."

She didn't pick up. Instead, he got her chirpy message telling him that she would love to talk to him but unfortunately couldn't take his call right now, blah, blah, blah. He stood there, watching as raindrops hit puddles and when the tone sounded for him to leave a message, he said: "Hailey. I need to talk to you. It's urgent."

Much as he was tempted to tell her to get away from Mr. Slick, and fast, he couldn't take the chance that he might somehow intercept the message.

He cursed.

If only she'd told him where she was going.

Fortunately her best friend Julia's business card was still in his wallet from when she'd first met him.

To his relief she answered right away. "First Impressions, Julia sp—"

"Julia, it's Rob. Hailey's in trouble."

"What?"

"I need to know where she is."

There was a pause and he got the feeling Hailey was one of those women who tell their BFF everything. Which was confirmed when Julia said carefully, "I'm sure if Hailey wanted you to know where she is she'd have told you."

Once more he had to tamp down the surge of emotions that threatened to choke him and make him do something stupid like scream at Julia.

"Listen. The guy she's with? I got a bad feeling about him. I snapped a few photos and sent them to a friend of mine who has connections. Turns out he's a real bad dude. We're talking international criminal here."

"Rob? Have you been drinking?"

"No. I'm serious. Please. Your friend is in real danger."

"I don't know."

"I'm a hard-news reporter. I have instincts honed by years of reporting on guys like him. And I have connections."

"Maybe I could just call her."

"I tried that. Her phone's off."

He heard her curse, knew she was worried about Hailey, but not sure whether it was her date or Rob who was the real problem.

How could Rob help her? Every second that ticked by was another second Hailey was at the scumbag's mercy. He said, "I'm going to give you the number of my editor at *World Week*. He'll confirm what I'm saying."

"How will I know it's really him?"

"You can look him up on Google!" Frustration careened through him. "Here's the number."

"Okay. I'm sorry to be difficult, but I have to look out for my friend."

"Then make sure you do. She's in real danger."

"WHAT'S UP?" John rolled over, lazily stroked Julia's back.

She snuggled up against him, glad to have his comfort and warmth. "That was the weirdest phone call." She relayed what Rob had said to her.

"You don't believe him?" he asked, frowning.

"I don't know. I don't want to cause Hailey any embarrassment."

She called her friend's cell. As Rob had told her, it was off. She left a message. "Hailey. It's Julia. Hope your date's going well. Call me the second you get this. Love you."

Then she rapidly texted a similar message.

"I didn't tell Rob where she is in case he's a crazy-ass stalker."

"What if he's telling the truth?"

She nibbled her lower lip. "He gave me his editor's phone number in New York. How do I even know it's his editor?"

"Seems like a pretty elaborate plan to get to a woman he sees almost every day anyway."

"I know. I just…" She turned to him, her new lover, and found there was something so reassuring and solid about him. It was wonderful to have a man she could trust. "The story seems so far-fetched. How many times does a girl end up on a date with a—a—terrorist?"

He drew her in close and kissed her cheek. "It seems to me that if there's even the smallest chance of it being true you need to warn her."

Julia jumped out of bed, grabbed her panties and stepped into them. "You're right. Come on, get dressed."

"I had plans for round two."

She dimpled at him. "Later. Right now you are taking me out to dinner at a very expensive new restaurant."

"Might this be the expensive new restaurant where your friend is on her date?"

"Yes."

He reached for his shirt. "So, we tell her she might want to ditch the date."

"You got it."

"And then round two?"

"And then round two."

"Are you going to tell Rob?"

"I don't think so. His instincts tell him this guy's bad news. Fair enough. But I have instincts, too, and they tell me that Rob crashing Hailey's date is a terrible idea."

HAILEY BELIEVED IN the power of positive thinking. And that meant that if she was determined to have a good time, she ought to have a good time.

The hollow feeling in her stomach must simply be hunger.

She pinned the bright smile back on her face as she listened to her date grill the wine waiter—no, sommelier, as he'd made a point to call him—about a certain vintage.

She suspected he was trying to impress her. She knew she should be flattered, but actually she was bored.

She didn't care about the microclimate where the grapes grew or the weather that summer or the phases of the moon when the fruit was harvested.

She liked to go to a restaurant, pick something that sounded good to eat, maybe have some wine and get on with it. She'd never been out with someone who took the menu apart and put it back together again and then approached the wine list—in this case an entire book—

like a battle of wits between him and the poor guy who simply wanted to take their wine order and move on.

This whole thing had been a bad idea. There was a reason, she reminded herself, why she never got involved with clients.

Gastronome, the trendy new eatery, was busy, but not crowded. The decor was sleek and modern. Her date had insisted on a table in a shadowed corner. "More private," he told her, touching her wrist. She'd smiled politely but didn't want to be private with him. She didn't even know him.

Once they were seated, he'd scanned the restaurant and she could have cursed Rob for putting stupid suspicions in her head. So what if Dennis preferred a dark corner, sat with his back to the wall and checked out the place with the vigilance of a spy who might need to make a quick getaway?

He was probably merely admiring the decor.

"Tell me why you chose Seattle?" she asked him once he'd finally approved the wine and she'd agreed with him that it was a very good vintage. As if she knew. Or cared.

"I'm ready to settle down," he said, relaxing back into his chair, sipping his wine. "This seems like a great city. It's cosmopolitan, but close to the outdoors. I like all the recreational opportunities. The climate's good. Mild."

She pointed to the picture window behind them where raindrops chased each other. "Except for all the rain."

"Yeah. First thing I'm going to do when I buy Bellamy House is hire an architect. I want a garage large enough for three cars."

"You're planning to tear the house down?"

"The value's in the land. And most of it is wasted on gardens and those trees. I'm going to build a place that has all the bells and whistles. Heated floors in all the bathrooms. Entire place wired for top-of-the-line electronics, home theater room, a gym." He sipped his wine thoughtfully, spinning the stem of the glass so the liquid swirled. "Temperature-controlled wine cellar, too."

"Wow. You have big plans."

"I've worked hard in my life. It's time to enjoy the rewards." He leaned closer to her. "And I'm definitely interested in finding someone to share my life with."

The gesture should have been sexy, but there was something calculated about it. He was good-looking, obviously rich, and someone who seemed to want what she wanted. A stable home life. Permanence.

She knew already there wouldn't be a second date.

And she strongly suspected there wouldn't be a home sale either. Once she told Rob about his plans to knock down Bellamy House she knew he'd never sell to this man.

In truth she didn't want Bellamy House to be redeveloped either. She loved the place. She'd grown to appreciate its quirky charm. And what of the garden where Agnes Neeson's ashes rested? Was Rob's grandmother going to end up underneath a home theater? The very notion was an outrage.

She glanced surreptitiously at her watch, wondering how soon she could eat her dinner and get out of here.

"You look so beautiful tonight," Dennis crooned. "That blue dress really brings out your eyes."

"Thank you." After the shopping trip with Julia had ended up in a long lunch and girl talk, she'd decided to forego a new outfit and wear one of her favorites. The blue silk was elegant without being overtly sexy. Dennis was a client, after all.

"And you're tall. I like a tall woman. I'm tall so we look good together."

Had he actually said that? And did she want a laundry list of obvious compliments?

She recalled the way Rob looked at her. He didn't gush about her eyes but his expression as he gazed at her made her feel beautiful.

Dennis Thurgood, by contrast, covered her in compliments the way a baker might cover a cake in sticky-sweet frosting. However, his eyes didn't warm when they looked at her. If anything he seemed to be calculating. How many years until her skin wrinkled? How well would she keep her slim figure after childbirth? She couldn't shake the notion that she was being studied and evaluated like the wine he'd chosen. Or the house he was planning to buy to raze and rebuild.

No, she thought, she really didn't want to be one of his possessions, like the original art he'd boasted of, the cars he'd described that would fill his garage and the rest of his carefully chosen possessions.

She wondered how she'd ever found him interesting.

And how soon she could make her escape.

20

ROB STOOD IN THE RAIN. Behind him the door of the bar opened periodically letting somebody in or out, along with a burst of bar noise. Once he heard a cheer.

He willed his cell to ring.

It remained stubbornly silent.

Julia should have figured out by now that he was telling the truth. Why hadn't she called him to tell him where Hailey was?

A cab pulled up and a young couple in jeans and raincoats made a run for the entrance. Before the cab drove away, Rob hailed it. Ran to the door and opened it. "You know the city well?"

The driver was between fifty and sixty with stubbled cheeks, a ball cap pulled low and eyes that had seen it all. "Yeah."

"What's the hot new restaurant in town?"

The guy shrugged. "Depends what you're looking for."

Rob climbed into the back of the cab. At least while he waited for his phone to ring, he could be doing something. "I'm meeting a woman at a restaurant and I can't remember the name of it." He held up his hands as if he were a typical, clueless dude.

"That sucks. She's waiting for you?"

"I think so."

The cabbie pulled out into traffic. "Why don't you call her?"

"I tried. Her phone's turned off. She's going to be pissed if I don't get there soon."

"Do you know anything about this place?"

He tried to think like a hardened criminal trying to pass as a normal guy. More than that, a catch. Rob recalled the expensive car the guy had rented, the designer duds, the Italian loafers. "Best restaurant in town that's also fairly new."

The driver reeled off a few names. Since he'd never heard the name of the restaurant they were of no use to Rob. "Of those, which one's the most expensive?"

"Oh," the driver said, catching his eye in the rearview mirror. "She's one of those women."

He shook his head. "You know, she's really not."

"Well, I'd say it's down to two. Gastronome or Luminous. Both are high-end. The first one I've heard has better food. Luminous is showier."

"Luminous. Let's try that one."

"You got it."

They headed downtown and hit traffic. Rob cursed every vehicle, every gnarl of construction, every fool who should be home and not out clogging the streets. Sweat crawled down his back as he imagined all the things a thug like Dennis Thurgood was capable of.

When they didn't move through an intersection in the space of two traffic lights, he banged his fist into his palm. "Come on!"

"This girl's really got to you."

"Yeah."

"You planning to propose tonight or something?"

As he sat there, pulled to knots by anxiety over this woman, Rob waited for the horror of the notion of marriage to sink in. It didn't. Instead he was struck by the rightness of the idea.

She belonged to him. He knew his famous instincts had been right about her date tonight, but what his famous instincts had forgotten to reveal was that he was miserable with jealousy, and that he and he alone, should be wining and dining Hailey. Wooing her—and there's a term his grandmother would have liked. Marrying her.

Now, all he had to do was find her, get her out of the clutches of a dangerous man and prove to her that he was the right man.

And he was determined to do that, if it took the rest of his life.

"I'm planning to marry her. If she'll have me." And the idea didn't stick in his throat. He had a book deal now. He could afford to spend more time at home.

After about ten million years of crawling through traffic, they finally arrived outside Luminous. "Hang here for just a sec," he snapped as he bolted from the cab.

He yanked open a heavy glass door, dashed inside, and knew almost instantly that he'd guessed wrong. The place was too brightly lit, and if a man had to make a quick exit, it was going to be difficult with all the columns and gold mirrors and what not.

"Just looking for a friend," he said as he jogged past the maître d' and in less than two minutes he was jogging back out. Back into the cab. "Nope. Let's try the other place."

They crawled back into heavy traffic. He groaned.

"How far is the other place?" he asked after five more minutes had moved at glacial speed and the cab had traveled ten feet.

"Three blocks that way." The driver pointed to his left.

"Okay. I'll walk it."

"Likely be faster."

He paid the guy and hopped out, heading in the direction indicated. Run a mile in six? The way his adrenaline was pumping he'd do it in four. He didn't care that his leg was sore. Didn't care rain was stinging his eyes and blurring his vision, didn't care that passersby glanced at him as though he was deranged.

He ran.

His leg burned, his lungs burned, every cell in his body pushed him forward. He had to get to her. Had to.

Common sense told him she couldn't be in any real danger, but common sense had no control over his gut instinct to get to her fast.

He jogged around a couple holding hands under matching umbrellas, dashed across a street against the light and got a screeching horn as a dark car seemed to come out of nowhere and slam on its brakes.

The driver rolled down the window and cursed fluently. He waved—in a kind of acknowledgment, apology, and *I don't have time to stop, this is an emergency* way—and kept running.

HAILEY WONDERED IF she'd ever been on a less successful date. Neither the exquisite food, nor the fancy wine, nor the discreet decor and exceptional service could change the fact that she didn't like her dining companion. He was boastful, rude to those he considered inferior, like the waiter, who looked as though he'd like to carve out her date's liver with a butter knife, and so full of sugary compliments to her that her teeth were starting to ache.

When they'd first arrived and been shown to their seats she'd surreptitiously scanned the place to see if there was anyone she recognized or anyone famous. But there was no one. So she was beyond surprised when an extremely familiar voice said, "Oh, my gosh, what a surprise!"

She glanced up.

"Julia!" If anyone was surprised, it was she. She'd told Julia not three hours ago when they'd had a wardrobe consultation, where she was going. Julia had declared her envy but made no mention of eating at the same restaurant tonight.

She wasn't even dressed for it. Julia, who always gowned herself in dramatic fashion, was wearing the same skirt and top she'd worn to work. Her lipstick was worn off and she had a bad case of bedhead. Her companion wasn't much better. He'd thrown a blazer over a denim shirt that was buttoned wrong, and he sported one blue sock and one brown.

Both of them had strange expressions on their faces. "Is something wrong?" she asked.

"No, of course not," Julia said, fake-casual. "I just—"

"Are these people your friends?" her date demanded.

"Yes. This is Julia Atkinson. The woman who staged Bellamy House. And her friend." She held out her hand. "I'm sorry, I've never met you. I'm Hailey."

"John. Pleasure." When she shook his hand, he squeezed. The guy either had some kind of neurological problem or he was trying to warn her about something. Based on the bizarre way these two were dressed and acting, she went with the latter.

When they were both introduced to her date, he sent them his bland smile and said, "Please. Join us."

"This is a table for two," she said, but he actually snapped his fingers at their waiter. "Two more chairs. Our friends will be joining us."

"Oh, no. Really…" Julia began.

"They probably want to be alone," she suggested.

"Nonsense. I insist. Dinner is my treat." As though money was everything. Or nothing.

They hovered, and then Julia said, "Could I talk to you for a minute in the bathroom?"

"Of cou—"

"Oh, I don't think that's a good idea at all," her date said. Still smiling, but with his teeth locked together. He put a hand on her arm to stop her from moving.

Hailey had had enough. Enough of being polite to this turkey, of spending time with a man she wasn't interested in, of men in general. She glared at her date. "Please take your hand off my arm."

His hand tightened. "You're causing a scene. Sit down. All of you."

There was something in his tone that made them all comply. She couldn't have described it without using hyperbole. *Deadly intent* was the closest she came. Which would be ridiculous if you hadn't noticed the utterly cold expression in his eyes.

"You two were obviously roused out of bed to come here," he said in that same cold tone.

"That's not—"

"Your clothes are a mess, your makeup is smudged and you have a hickey on your neck."

"I had a busy day, I—"

His voice sliced through Julia's words. "Cut the crap. Why are you here?"

Hailey glanced up and saw a sight that made her heart leap. Heading toward them was Rob. He was soaked to the skin, his leg a little stiff so she knew it was paining him. From the way he was panting he'd been running.

She had never been so happy to see anyone. In that moment their gazes connected and she saw such fierce, passionate love in the depths of his eyes she wondered how she had ever doubted his feelings.

As he closed in on their table, he said, "Why don't you cut the crap?" to her dinner date.

"What the hell's going on here?" Dennis asked. His expression was hard suddenly, his eyes scanning the area behind Rob. It was as though a mask had fallen off. The smug, look-how-rich-and-successful-I-am, I-want-to-settle-down-and-I-might-choose-you act was gone. As she stared at the cold, hard man, she wondered how she'd ever thought him charming. Or good-looking. What she saw in his face made her skin prickle.

Rob looked tougher than she'd ever seen him. "Let's just say your date is over. Come on, Hailey." He held out his hand to her. There were so many messages he was trying to send her, but she only received one. Loud and clear. *Come now, I'll explain later.*

Oh, and I love you.

Julia and John were already rising, Hailey started to stand, held out her hand to Rob. Soon she'd be out of here.

In that brief second before they could reach each other, another hand clamped on her arm.

Again.

She did not like being manhandled, she did not like having spent an awful evening with a crummy date and she most of all did not like the knowledge that something bad was happening and she had no idea what.

She bared her teeth and swung around to Dennis. "Let go of me."

To her fury, he didn't let go. He tightened his grip and yanked her hard so she lost her balance in the damn high heels she'd worn, hit her hip on the table and fell into his lap, knocking most of his glass of wine on top of both of them.

She tried to scramble up, saw Rob coming for her, and then out of the corner of her eye saw the flash of black metal.

A gun.

21

"OH, SHIT," ROB SAID when he saw the gun and stopped in his tracks, his hands clenching at his sides, even as she felt the hard metal press into her side.

"Sit. Down," Dennis said to Julia and John.

Julia looked as though she were going to cry. She sat. John sat.

Dennis Thurgood motioned Rob to Hailey's now-vacant chair.

Rob hesitated, and then sat.

She could feel the tension in Dennis in the rigidity of his muscles. Otherwise he seemed cool and unruffled, as though he took his dates hostage by gunpoint all the time.

His calmness was almost as frightening as the gun.

The wine seeping through her skirt made her skin sticky.

"What we're going to do is leave this restaurant together. You—" he nodded to Rob "—go first. Open the door for all of us. You two go next. Hailey and I will exit last. I'm sure I don't need to tell you to act normal. I wouldn't want anybody to get hurt."

"Then what?" Rob demanded. "After we're outside, then what?"

"I will take my date home like a gentleman. And you three have a nice night."

"I don't—"

She gasped as the man with the gun jabbed it into her ribs.

"This is not negotiable."

"Okay," Rob said. "Okay."

Rob got up slowly. Began to walk to the door.

"Now you two," Dennis said.

Julia and John rose and followed Rob. John reached for Julia's hand and clasped it.

"Now get up slowly and don't do anything stupid. I am in no mood to dispose of a body tonight. Understand?"

She nodded. It was awkward getting out from behind the table with the gun and the man both pressing against her. She felt angry and helpless. She couldn't imagine a worse combination.

Her eyes searched desperately for their waiter. If there was one person who'd love to cause this guy trouble, it had to be him. He was nowhere to be seen.

She felt sweat prickle at her hairline, tried to make eye contact with other diners, staff, anyone. However, it was one of those discreet places where every diner had the illusion of privacy and the staff did their best to be invisible.

Great. Just great.

Rob was ahead of them, taking his sweet time getting to the door. John and Julia were following his pace. Her heart was beating uncomfortably fast and she felt as though she couldn't breathe.

The hand holding the gun was rock-steady. The notion that he'd killed before crossed her mind, only to be banished. She'd end up a blithering basket case if she let herself think like that. She had to keep her wits about her. She wasn't alone.

She wasn't alone.

Even if this turned out to be the last evening of her life she had the blinding realization that she wasn't a rootless army brat anymore. She had Julia, a friend so firm that she'd risk her life for her friend.

And she had Rob. For as long or as short as their future might be, she knew that he loved her and that he'd do anything to keep her safe.

Her eyes threatened to mist as she discovered she already had what she'd been looking for. A home. People she could count on.

Roots.

And no creepy, self-centered, gun-toting thug was going to take that away from her.

There was a way. There had to be. Somebody would see them, he'd lose his focus for a moment. That's all it would take.

Even as she had the thought, one of the waitstaff stopped playing by the invisible rule. And, thank God, it was their waiter.

"Excuse me, sir. I think you forgot to pay your bill," he said in a loud voice.

Yes!

She felt her companion go absolutely rigid. As she'd guessed he'd completely forgotten they hadn't paid yet.

Then he turned them both. She could feel him put on his fake smarm act. "My girlfriend's not feeling well. Let me get her outside for some air. I'll be right back."

The waiter glanced at her and she widened her eyes trying to yell "Help!" without saying a word.

He looked more skeptical than heroic. As if they were dine-and-dash artists who pulled stunts like this all the time. Her evening went down another notch, if it was possible.

"Her friends could take her outside while you take care of the bill," the waiter said. As she'd hoped the commotion had caused a few of the diners to start paying attention. If anything at least now people had a reason to remember them.

Rob had stopped inside the door, Julia and John standing with him.

Two older women had finished paying and were rising from their table, handbags in hand.

Rob said something to Julia and John and began to push open the door.

A chorus of sirens penetrated the quiet restaurant as the door opened.

She felt the change in her captor. His heart began to bang and his breath came in harsh pulls. "Shut that door and get back inside," he snarled.

John shut the door and maneuvered himself so he was standing in front of Julia.

The older women headed for the front desk, their coat-check slips in their hands.

"Sit back down," Dennis ordered them.

One turned, a silver-haired elegant woman wearing a black suit and pearls the size of gumballs. "I beg your pardon?"

"I said sit down." And he pulled out the gun for all to see.

The woman looked at him for a steady second, then

said in a firm tone pitched loud enough that Hailey suspected her friend was hard of hearing, "Come on, Mavis. I think we'd better sit down."

The other woman had her back to them. "But we've got ballet tickets, and I am *not* missing the opening." And she continued on her way.

For a second, the awful pressure of the gun pressing into her was relieved. She barely had time to shut her eyes and scrunch her shoulders when the gun blasted.

A big chunk of plaster rained down from the ceiling.

The woman referred to as Mavis shrieked and turned.

"You're not going anywhere. This restaurant is in lockdown." Then Dennis began hauling Hailey backward, away from the front door and Rob, back to the kitchen.

"Those of you pulling out your cell phones, don't forget to tell the cops I have a hostage."

He dragged her back, even as the older woman with the pearls said, "You'll never get away with this."

Hailey searched for Rob, wanting the reassurance of seeing his face, but to her dismay, he was ducking out of the front door.

No, she silently cried. *Don't do it, Rob. Don't be a hero.*

She knew in that moment that he was going to try and run around the building and cut them off. However, he was an unarmed man with an injured leg. Her captor was a hardened criminal with his own gym and the definite advantage of a handgun.

He was so familiar with his way to the back entrance to the restaurant that she had to assume he'd checked out the layout before he ever made a reservation here. She wondered what it would be like to live like that, always ready to run. Ready to kill. Never entering a front door until you knew how to get out the back.

The hallway bypassed the kitchen, where, from the bustle and sounds of pots banging and food sizzling, she had to assume the drama playing out in the front hadn't penetrated. He dragged her down the hall, past the bathrooms and a storage closet to a fire door.

"Open the door," he snapped.

No one had followed them though she had to believe police and help were on their way. For now it was only the two of them here. She had no options.

She pushed the metal bar of the fire door and eased it open.

He held her and peeked around her shoulder, shielding himself with her body in the reverse fashion to John and Julia.

No flashing police cars greeted them. The lot was quiet. His car was exactly where he'd left it.

"Head for the car." He hit the button on the keypad that unlocked his fancy rental. "You'll be driving."

As she began to move to the car she heard the scuffling of shoes and Rob came running around the corner toward them.

"What the—"

"Dennis!" Rob yelled. "Leave her behind. Take me instead."

"Why would I do that?"

"Because I'm a high-profile guy. My company would do a lot to make sure I was safe. I'm a media personality. You can use that as leverage to get away."

"Why don't I take you both?"

"It's not practical," Rob was panting from the effort of getting here so fast.

"You don't have time to secure one of us and two hostages put you in more danger. You know that."

"Come closer, let me see you."

"No, Rob. Don't," she cried, feeling her captor's hatred for the man she loved.

Rob was walking forward, hands held up and high as though he were surrendering.

"That guy really pisses me off," Dennis Thurgood said and fired.

"No," she screamed, even as the bullet hit Rob in the chest, knocking him down and backward.

As the man she loved hit the dirt, something snapped inside her. A terrible scream was ripped from her throat and anger so red and hot rushed through her that she had no conscious thought—only action. She grabbed his gun hand before Dennis could fire again, squeezing it with both hands, driving her knee up into his groin with every bit of adrenaline-fired strength in her body. She caught him off guard and he grunted and swayed but didn't let go of the gun.

They wrestled for it, and she knew her superstrength couldn't last for long and he'd only be incapacitated for a few seconds. She had to get that gun. She bared her teeth and fastened them onto his wrist like a frenzied pit bull.

She had no thought of her own safety, was only determined that he wouldn't get a chance to hurt Rob anymore.

Rob wasn't dead. He wouldn't be dead. He couldn't be. Life without Rob was not an option. And she was going to put everything she had on the line, including her life, to make sure that Dennis didn't have a chance to finish him.

He kicked her but she didn't let go. She tasted blood and bit down harder. If she could just get the gun out of his hand....

Suddenly she wasn't alone anymore.

A shadow appeared in her peripheral vision. There was movement. Impact.

Dennis gave a grunt and the gun dropped.

"You can let go of his arm now," Rob said gently.

She did. Realized Rob was standing with the gun trained on Dennis who was sagging against the nearest car.

She took a few steps away from him, tried to figure out how Rob could be standing, decided that believing in miracles was a healthy option and bent over to draw in some deep breaths.

Rob pulled out his cell phone. She heard him say, "The fugitive has been subdued, the hostage is safe. The man holding the gun is friendly. Understood?"

And within minutes, all the sirens and flashing lights she could have wished for converged.

Rob was quickly relieved of the gun, her client/date/kidnapper was led away in handcuffs. While a number of people in various uniforms were suddenly swarming, giving orders, asking questions, Rob put up a hand. Turned to her.

He took a step forward. She took one and suddenly they were in each other's arms. As she grabbed him tightly into a hug he winced.

"Oh, I forgot. He shot you. How did you..."

He lifted his shirt and she saw the dark vest. "Kevlar," he said. "I wear it in the field. Decided to throw it on tonight. Most of the time you don't need them, but once in a while—"

"They can save your life."

She touched the spot where the bullet had hit. "You'd have been killed."

"Probably."

Her eyes filled. The stress and pent-up anger and fear of the evening roared up. "What would I ever do without you?"

"Hailey, God willing, you are never going to have to find out."

As she looked up, she found him smiling down at her and then they were kissing, hungrily.

Yes, everything inside her shouted. This was so right. Yes.

"WE'LL WORK IT OUT," he said, holding her so tight she could feel that he was trembling, too. "I got a book deal. I can stay home more."

"I love you enough to let you go."

"And about Bellamy House…"

"I don't think Dennis Thurgood is going to buy it," she said, with a faint laugh that would go hysterical if she wasn't very careful.

"Nobody's going to buy it," he informed her.

Hope filled all the places where fear had lived a few seconds ago. "No?"

"I'm taking it off the market. I'm keeping it."

"Oh, Rob."

"I don't know exactly how all this is going to work. But I'm not losing you. I can't lose you."

"But your job…"

"It's only a job. The thing is, I thought I was like my mother. I thought I couldn't settle down. But I'm not. I was running away. I've been running away since

I was fourteen years old." He touched her face where a raindrop skidded down her cheek. "I don't need to run anymore."

"Mr. Klassen?" a uniformed cop asked, coming close.

"Yes."

"We're going to need to talk to you both down at the station. Get your statements."

"Tonight?" Rob turned, looking tired and frustrated. "Can't it wait until the morning?"

"I'm sorry sir, but—"

"Of course it can wait until the morning," a firm and somewhat familiar voice said.

Hailey stared to see the elegant woman with the pearls step carefully over the puddles to reach them.

"I'm Judge Eleanor Hanover," she said. She handed them each a business card. "We've got plenty of reasons to hold that man in custody. Let these two get some well-earned rest."

"Of course, Your Honor."

"Thank you," Hailey said.

She smiled at them. "That was quite an eventful evening. If you could come by the precinct at nine o'clock?"

They both nodded. She couldn't imagine arguing with this woman.

Julia and John arrived next.

Julia grabbed her friend in a hug so tight Hailey's ribs threatened to crack. "Oh, honey. I am so glad you're okay."

"Me, too."

"And Rob. I'm sorry I didn't believe you. Exactly."

A wry grin twisted his mouth. "You were looking after your friend. I get that."

"No hard feelings?"

He shook his head. Julia put out her arms to hug him.

"Not too hard," Hailey warned. "He got shot."

"Again?"

"It's kind of a bad habit," Hailey said, on another hysterical giggle.

"One that's going to stop," Rob promised.

"We haven't met. I'm John."

The men shook hands.

And then they stood there. The sirens were muted. Most of the cop cars had left. Dennis Thurgood had been taken away.

"Do you need a ride home?" John asked.

"Yeah. Actually, we do," Rob said.

On the way home Hailey demanded to be told the whole story. Between getting three different versions of the tale, she finally pieced together that Rob's instincts had been right all along; that Julia was the best friend she'd ever had and that John was Julia's perfect match.

It felt like the middle of the night when they reached Bellamy House, but when she checked her watch it was only a little after eleven. The stress had exhausted her.

She and Rob pretty much helped each other up the stairs into the master bedroom.

When Rob undressed, she cried out when she saw the bruise already spreading where the bullet had hit the vest. One more wound for a man who couldn't help being a hero.

She kissed the spot.

And he kissed her wrist where Thurgood had left bruises.

They lay together, simply holding each other. Hearing him breathe was such a gift, knowing he was warm and alive and hers, at least for now.

"Rob," she said after a while.

"Mmm?"

"I love you."

"I know."

Her eyes prickled. "I love you enough to let you go."

He turned to her and she saw again the depths of his feelings for her. "And I love you enough to stay."

"But—"

"I didn't have time to tell you about it, but I've been working on this idea. How all over the world, people have the same problems. They may be different colors and live in mud huts or McMansions but deep down we live similar lives. Where to live? How to earn a living? Courting, raising kids. It's mostly told through pictures. My agent said Fremont comes across like one of the characters. And I realized that I do have a home. I've always had a home. I just never had a strong enough reason to stay." He touched her face. "Until now."

"But your work—"

"Well, first I'll be writing about a certain arms dealer. A *World Week* exclusive." He chuckled. "Gary will love it. That's my editor. And they want me to write some features around the book. I've got a big enough advance that I can afford to take some more time here."

He touched her breast and she sighed. "You're firing me again, aren't you?"

He chuckled. "Yeah. I guess I am. I'll make up your commission somehow."

She let her own hands wander. Felt his arousal. "How?"

"I could give you half of Bellamy House." Her hand clutched so suddenly he winced. "Are you saying…"

"That I want to marry you? Yes."

"Oh, Rob." They kissed for a long time, and then she said, "I am such a good Realtor. I always end up with the right people for a house."

"I don't have all the answers yet, but we'll work it out. If we love each other, we'll work it out."

"Do we?" she smiled at him tenderly. "Love each other enough?"

He traced her lips with his fingertip. "Oh, yeah," he said, and then he pulled her against him.

* * * * *

COMING NEXT MONTH from Harlequin® Blaze™
AVAILABLE SEPTEMBER 18, 2012

#711 BLAZING BEDTIME STORIES, VOLUME IX
Bedtime Stories
Rhonda Nelson and Karen Foley
Two of Harlequin Blaze's bestselling authors invite you to curl up in bed with their latest collection of sensual fairy tales, guaranteed to inspire sweet—and *very* sexy—dreams!

#712 THE MIGHTY QUINNS: CAMERON
The Mighty Quinns
Kate Hoffmann
Neither Cameron Quinn nor FBI agent Sophie Reyes is happy hanging out in Vulture Creek, New Mexico. But when Cameron helps Sophie on a high profile case, he realizes that sexy Sophie has stolen his heart.

#713 OWN THE NIGHT
Made in Montana
Debbi Rawlins
Jaded New Yorker Alana Richardson wants to go a little country with Blackfoot Falls sheriff Noah Calder. He just needs to figure out if she belongs in his bed...or in jail!

#714 FEELS SO RIGHT
Friends With Benefits
Isabel Sharpe
Physical therapist Demi Anderson knows she has the right job when the world's sexiest man walks into her studio, takes off his shirt and begs her to help him. Colin Russo needs Demi's healing touch...but having her hands on him is sweet torture!

#715 LIVING THE FANTASY
Kathy Lyons
Ali Flores has never believed in luck, until she accidentally lands a part on a video game tour. Now she's learning all about gaming. But what she *really* likes is playing with hunky company CEO Ken Johnson....

#716 FOLLOW MY LEAD
Stepping Up
Lisa Renee Jones
The host and one of the judges of TV's hottest reality dance show put the past behind them and embark on a sensually wild, emotionally charged fling!

You can find more information on upcoming Harlequin® titles, free excerpts and more at www.Harlequin.com.

HBCNM0912

REQUEST YOUR FREE BOOKS!
2 FREE NOVELS PLUS 2 FREE GIFTS!

red-hot reads!

YES! Please send me 2 FREE Harlequin® Blaze™ novels and my 2 FREE gifts (gifts are worth about $10). After receiving them, if I don't wish to receive any more books, I can return the shipping statement marked "cancel." If I don't cancel, I will receive 6 brand-new novels every month and be billed just $4.49 per book in the U.S. or $4.96 per book in Canada. That's a saving of at least 14% off the cover price. It's quite a bargain. Shipping and handling is just 50¢ per book in the U.S. and 75¢ per book in Canada.* I understand that accepting the 2 free books and gifts places me under no obligation to buy anything. I can always return a shipment and cancel at any time. Even if I never buy another book, the two free books and gifts are mine to keep forever.

151/351 HDN FEQE

Name _____ (PLEASE PRINT)

Address _____ Apt. #

City _____ State/Prov. _____ Zip/Postal Code

Signature (if under 18, a parent or guardian must sign) _____

Mail to the **Reader Service:**
IN U.S.A.: P.O. Box 1867, Buffalo, NY 14240-1867
IN CANADA: P.O. Box 609, Fort Erie, Ontario L2A 5X3

Not valid for current subscribers to Harlequin Blaze books.

Want to try two free books from another line?
Call 1-800-873-8635 or visit www.ReaderService.com.

* Terms and prices subject to change without notice. Prices do not include applicable taxes. Sales tax applicable in N.Y. Canadian residents will be charged applicable taxes. Offer not valid in Quebec. This offer is limited to one order per household. All orders subject to credit approval. Credit or debit balances in a customer's account(s) may be offset by any other outstanding balance owed by or to the customer. Please allow 4 to 6 weeks for delivery. Offer available while quantities last.

Your Privacy—The Reader Service is committed to protecting your privacy. Our Privacy Policy is available online at www.ReaderService.com or upon request from the Reader Service.

We make a portion of our mailing list available to reputable third parties that offer products we believe may interest you. If you prefer that we not exchange your name with third parties, or if you wish to clarify or modify your communication preferences, please visit us at www.ReaderService.com/consumerchoice or write to us at Reader Service Preference Service, P.O. Box 9062, Buffalo, NY 14269. Include your complete name and address.

HB11B

HARLEQUIN Blaze™
red-hot reads

Two sizzling fairy tales with men straight from your wildest dreams...

Fan-favorite authors

Rhonda Nelson & Karen Foley

bring readers another installment of

Blazing Bedtime Stories, Volume IX

THE EQUALIZER

Modern-day righter of wrongs, Robin Sherwood is a man
on a mission and will do everything necessary to see that
through, especially when that means catching
the eye of a fair maiden.

GOD'S GIFT TO WOMEN

Sculptor Lexi Adams decides there is no such thing as the
perfect man, until she catches sight of Nikos Christakos,
the sexy builder next door. She convinces herself that she
only wants to sculpt him, but soon finds a cold stone
statue is a poor substitute for the real deal.

Available October 2012 wherever books are sold.

New York Times *bestselling author Brenda Jackson*
presents TEXAS WILD,
a brand-new Westmoreland novel.

Available October 2012 from Harlequin Desire®!

Rico figured there were a lot of things in life he didn't know. But the one thing he did know was that there was no way Megan Westmoreland was going to Texas with him. He was attracted to her, big-time, and had been from the moment he'd seen her at Micah's wedding four months ago. Being alone with her in her office was bad enough. But the idea of them sitting together on a plane or in a car was arousing him just thinking about it.

He could tell by the mutinous expression on her face that he was in for a fight. That didn't bother him. Growing up, he'd had two younger sisters to deal with, so he knew well how to handle a stubborn female.

She crossed her arms over her chest. "Other than the fact that you prefer working alone, give me another reason I can't go with you."

He crossed his arms over his own chest. "I don't need another reason. You and I talked before I took this case, and I told you I would get you the information you wanted… doing things my way."

He watched as she nibbled on her bottom lip. So now she was remembering. Good. Even so, he couldn't stop looking into her beautiful dark eyes, meeting her fiery gaze head-on.

"As the client, I demand that you take me," she said.

He narrowed his gaze. "You can demand all you want, but you're not going to Texas with me."

Megan's jaw dropped. "I *will* be going with you since there's no good reason that I shouldn't."

He didn't say anything for a moment. "Okay, there is another reason I won't take you with me. One that you'd do well to consider," he said in a barely controlled tone. She had pushed him, and he didn't like being pushed.

"Fine, let's hear it," she snapped furiously.

He placed his hands in the pockets of his jeans, stood with his legs braced apart and leveled his gaze on her. "I want you, Megan. Bad. And if you go anywhere with me, I'm going to have you."

He then turned and walked out of her office.

Will Megan go to Texas with Rico?

Find out in Brenda Jackson's brand-new Westmoreland novel, TEXAS WILD.

Available October 2012 from Harlequin Desire®.

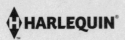

HARLEQUIN®

n o c t u r n e™

Satisfy your paranormal cravings with two dark
and sensual new werewolf tales from
Harlequin® Nocturne™!

FOREVER WEREWOLF
by Michele Hauf

Can sexy, charismatic werewolf Trystan Hawkes win the
heart of Alpine pack princess Lexi Connors—or will dark
family secrets cost him the pack's trust…and her love?

THE WOLF PRINCESS
by Karen Whiddon

Will Dr. Braden Streib risk his life to save royal wolf shifter
Princess Alisa—even if it binds them inescapably together
in a battle against a deadly faction?

Plus look for a reader-favorite story
included in each book!

2 GREAT NOVELS
SAME GREAT PRICE

Available September 18, 2012

HN88555